The Diary
of Delia

The Diary of Delia

Onoto Watanna

MINT EDITIONS

The Diary of Delia was first published in 1907.

This edition published by Mint Editions 2021.

ISBN 9781513271583 | E-ISBN 9781513276588

Published by Mint Editions®

 MINT
EDITIONS

minteditionbooks.com

Publishing Director: Jennifer Newens
Design & Production: Rachel Lopez Metzger
Project Manager: Micaela Clark
Typesetting: Westchester Publishing Services

Contents

I

I got up at siven. Washed. Dressed. Made me bed. I set the kittle on the gas stove and then furyissly rung the brikfust bell. The famly begun to get up about 9. Mr. John was the first to ate. He guv a look sideways at the appytising eggs befure him and the luvly staming coffee and thin wid a shuv pooshed thim aside. He tuk up his paper and begun to reed ignoaring me and the brikfust as if we wus durt. Me mouth being open I spoke up.

"Won't you be after ating this morning" says I.

"Its all rite" says he. "Its all rite Delia."

I lingered hoping to help him a bit. He russelled up the paper the way he has of doing when provoaked and says in that cam and gintle way he talks when turribly excited:

"Delia—what are you waiting for?"

"Nothing—says I—but won't you be ating a bite Mr. Johnny."

He controlled himsilf wid diffyculty his voyce all the cammer for his inwurd anger.

Now me girl says he—you attind to your own ating. Never mind me.

I shugged me sholders in the disdainful way I have and walked kitchen-wurd. I'd jest reeched the swinging door when "Delia!" ses he, calling very perlitely now.

"Well sir?"

"Will you kindly bring me" ses he "a cup of hot water."

"Hot water is it?"

"Yep. I'm dying Delia" ses he.

"Dying!" ses I, shocked so that I drapped and broke the china in me hands.

"Confound you!" ses he, starting up in his seet "Dy-et-ing I said."

"Its the same thing!" I showted back at him, and I marched out in a huff.

By and by I heard Miss Claire go into the dining-room and I let her ring the table bell awile befure ansering. Her payshunce gitting the better of her sense she pokes her hed into me kitchen. Now I happened to be standing neerby the dure, wayting for further ivints. Well, as I sed, out popped Miss Claire's hed throo the dure which banged against me own, while me frying-pan wint flying up on hers.

"O! O! O!" crys she.

Her mother come running down the passage in her nitegown her hair scrooed up in them kid curlers.

"What is the matter?" crys she. Thin she seen the cundition of her dorter. The eggs had landed on her hed, and the fat run down her face in streams wid the yokes for company. The mother guv me a shove, and at that I boorst out in me rarth.

"Its no lady you are" ses I. "The whole boonch of you is bad. Gitting up at these unairthly ours and bullying the life out of a poor loan hard working girl."

Wid that I tuk aff me aprun and throwed it at the madams feet.

"Will you be good enuff" ses I "to pay me me wages, for I'm for going."

"Delia" ses she in the voyce she spakes whin drissed up fine for the opery or there's company for dinner. "Delia" ses she, "Your month is up on the 24th. You will get nothing till then."

"Indade" ses I, "Then I'll set here till the 24th, but divil a bit of work will I be doing," and wid that I set down on me chare and faulded me arms firmly across me brist.

"Delia" ses the lady, "Mr. Wolley will want his chop in a minit. Master Willie will have fareena and a poched egg. Shedded weet biskits for Miss Claire—"

"Mummer" ses she, washing her hed over me tubs, "I want nothing—nothing."

Just then Mr. James wint into the dyning-roon and rung the bell lowdly.

"Peeches and pancakes" ses Mrs. Wolley coldly.

Miss Claire has her hed washed be this time, and she stands oop, wid it rolled oop in a towel. She guv me wan look—a cross betwane a shmile and a frown, and ses she:

"Delia, do you wish *me* to get brikfust to-day?"

"God forbid, Miss" ses I, and wint to wark.

Miss Claire is horty agin, and she ses wid a cold look at me:

"Very well thin Delia, till the 24th then. Come mother."

II

Next Day

Its a weery world. Here I be, a poor loansome female alone in this crool city warking for foaks wid lether harts.

"O wirra, wirra, wirra" as me auld mother used to say.

Aroze. Dressed. Washed.

I wint to see me frind Minnie Carnavan last nite and feel better the day. Ses she:

"Its a fool you be Delia O'Mally. The Idear of you doing all the wark in a family of 6. Its no more sinse you seem to have than an eediot. Delia ses she, its the gurls thats been here long thats foolish like yursilf. They get stook wid wan famly who hangs on to thim for deer life. The new wans—green from the auld cuntry arent hiring out to do gineral housewark. Its cooking in a family of 1 or 2 theyre looking for and getting. Its lite chamberwark or waiting on a table or the like. Theres never a one so green as to hire out to do the hole wark of a family. Your auld fashuned and saft" ses she, "Go down to Mack's on 3rd Ave. Git a job for a munth or so as capper."

"And what is that?"

"Well you tak a job" ses Minnie, "but you don't kape it."

"And what wud be the sinse of taking it for thin?"

"Why you gump for ivery place you tak Mack gits a fee of $3. You get harf for fooling thim."

"Its an onest gurl I am" ses I wid scorn, "and its ashamed I'd be to mix mesilf in any such mess as that."

"Well then" ses she "go down to the Alluyance. Its a place where they get jobs for the rich."

"And what wud I be doing there?"

"Don't you mind what I'm after meening? Its the rich ladies who pathronize them. Its a foine thing indade for thim. The Alluyunce fills oop there houses wid the sarvants. If a lady walks in modestly asking swately for a gurl for gineral housewark, they taks the fee of two or three or maybe five dollars, and thin smilingly infarm her that gineral housewarkers are an oonown quolity. 'Tak a cook' ses Miss Flimflam, seeted at a desk. 'But' ses the lady, luking very thrubbled, 'a cook wont do anny other work at all.'"

"Sumtimes they do lite londry wark." ses Miss Flimflam, yoning perlitely in her hand.

"Will they clean?"

"Land no!"

"Wate on table?"

"Certainly not."

"Thin" ses the lady in disthress, "What am I to do? I moost have me wark dun."

"Why" ses the clerk, a little more awake, "hire other girls, as the rist of our pathrons do."

"Oh" ses the lady. "I suppose" ses she after a moment of deep and thrubbled thort, "if I get an exthra woman in to clean and wate on table the cook will wark cheeper?"

"Hm?" ses the lady at the disk. "I big yure pardin?"

"She'd wark cheeper, I sed?"

"Well to be frank, Mrs. Hodge Podge" answers Miss Flimflam at the desk, "a cooks an expinsive proppysition in these days. Now we have thim all the way down from $200 a munth to—er—well, you mite git an inexeperienced beginnir for about $30, tho I cant promise."

"Your fooling Minnie. Shure no cook gits such a forchune" ses I.

"Its thruth I'm telling you. Why I heard the uther day that Mrs. Vanderfool do be paying her cook $20,000 a year, and whats more the papers state theres an agytation now on foot among the bizzy club wimmin to let the poor hard warking girls, whose been imposaed upon for sinturies, yuse the parlor wance a week to see there company in."

"You don't say" ses I, "and to think of me drudging for the starving wage of $20 per month."

"Well" ses Minnie, "I wont misguide you Delia. $20 is the wages of a green girl who niver saw a Frinch pertater fryed on airth and who broils a stake in a sorspan cuvered snug wid water."

III

The Twenty-Fourth

I aroze at the ushil our. Washed. Dressed in me best. Miss Claire cum into me room brite and airly. Ses she: "O Delia, heres that auld green skurt of mine you always liked. Your welcome to it."

"Thanks" ses I, "but I expect to be making sooch grand wages soon, Miss Claire, I'll be bying finer skurts than that." Wid that I pushed the skurt aside with contemshus tooch.

She got all red and pretty, as she has a habit whin angry, and she put up her hed hy in the air.

"O well, if that's the way you feel!" ses she and marched out.

Mr. John cum into me kitchen.

"Delia" ses he "heres a quarter. Now hussle wid me brikfust, will you?"

I took the quarter and flipped it round.

"Mr. Johnny" ses I, "me munth is oop at 7 A.M. this morning. I'm after waiting for me wages."

He drew up his brows frowning and wint aff into his mothers room.

A moment later the auld gintleman himsilf cum bloostering out. Its his ushil custum to get up at 10.

"Whats up! Whats up!" ses he.

"Wheres me chop? Wheres me chop?"

Master Will started in to ball and Mr. James kept ringing the table bell. Such a house I never seen. Out came the madame in her ushil nitegown.

"Delia" ses she "didn't I tell you yesterday I'd decided to guv you anuther chance."

"You did mam, but I'm for going now" ses I.

"Go about your wark" ses she, her proud voice becoming a bit narvous in toan.

"I'm waiting for me wages mam" ses I.

"Delia—" she guv a hasty look about her, thin she spakes in a coaxing vyce:

"Now Delia, be sinsible. You no we think warlds of you. Now—"

Joost then, Miss Claire looks in, her face still red wid the snub I'm after giving her about the skurt.

"Muther" ses she, "don't descind to begging Delia to remane. *Let* her go. We can get on famissly widout her."

"What!" shourts Mr. James, sticking in his hed at the dure, "No cook! Whats to becum of us. Are we" ses he "to go throo a like nitemare such as we injured befure the advent of Delia?"

Willie now cum poking *his* hed in between his daddy's legs.

"Pleese Delia" ses he "guv me my fareena. *I* love you, Delia" ses he.

"God love the lamb!" ses I and flew to the stove, me hart going out of me body to the child.

"Hold!" ses Miss Claire, very loftily, and she cum over to me and tuk the dubble boyler out of me hand. "Put on yure things" ses she "and go. At *once*" ses she "at once!"

Then she turned to her brothers and parents.

"Go back to the dining-room" ses she "*I'll* get brikfust to-day."

Mr. James guv a dridful groan, and sloonk off to the dining-room, wid his hands on his stummick.

"Mamma" ses Miss Claire, "pay off Delia. Youve been composed upon long enuff" ses she. "Hereafter *I'll* manage things."

And me, the last of 1,700 girls in the same place—for so I larned from me frind the janitor's wife—walked out wid me $20 in me pocket.

IV

The Following Day at Minnie Carnavan's House

A roze at 8:30. Washed—all over. Dressed in me best. Borrowed Minnie's hat wid the grand white ostrich fether. Minnie wint along wid me to the Alluyunce. "For" ses she "its saft you are, mavorneen."

After paying our fee of $1 we set around thegither wid mebbe 40 uther unforchnut girls in a room on the sicond flure. "Now remimber" ses Minnie, "no *gineral* housewark for you. Its a grand cook you be, or a foine first-class waitress, or an illigunt chamber-made, or a nurse to a babby oonderstanding all about bottle feeding. Now raymimber what you are."

"I begin to have mis doubts, Minnie" ses I, trimbling inwardly.

"Ah go wan" ses Minnie, wid contimp, and just thin wan of the Miss Flimflams (for so Minnie had them all named), cum into the room and ses in a loud voyce:

"A nurse! I've a call here for a nurse. Must be first-class. Consumtive. Wages $10 a week."

"Tak it!" wispers Minnie, excitedly and she pushed me along.

"Are you a nurse?" arsks Miss Flimflam, looking at me misdoubtfully.

"Well mam" ses I "Its manny a yung wan—"

"O deer!" ses she impayshuntly, "a *trayned* nurse is what I want. Are there any trayned nurses here?"

There wint a little pockmarked woman forward.

"What have you dun?" arsks Miss Flimflam.

"Well deerie" ses the pockmarked lady, "I've tinded to invaleeds since I was so high deerie. Me speshultys obstetery."

"Obstetery? Whats that?" arsks Miss Flimflam opening oop her eyes wide.

"Why I'm a midwife, to spake voolgarly deerie" ses the pockmarked wan.

"Oh" ses Miss Flimflam, and wint out larfing.

Shed been gone but a minit whin a stout miss Flimflam cums in in a hurry. She reeds frum a paper in her hand:

"2 lady's maids, bootler, 3 chamber-mades—cook—in fack all necessary sarvants for a big coontry place. Now first of all—a thoruly first-class cook—er—"

Minnie had pushed me forward and I wint up bashfully befure her.

"Cum along" ses she, and she tuk me down stares into a grate long room, wid about twinty or thirty ladies sitting in grand drisses on sofies. She leeds me up to a stout old-yung lady sitting forward on the idge of wan of the sofies. "This" ses Miss Flimflam in the swatest voyce, "is Mrs. Regal. Tell her all about yersilf Delia."

The lady sits a bit further forward and lifts up wan of thim spicticles on top of a reel gold shtick called in Frinch Lorgons.

"How old are you?" ses she.

"Twinty" ses I.

"—five" puts in Minnie quickly, for she'd cum down wid me.

"Ah 25. How minny yeers have you cooked?"

"Well mam—" I began, whin Minnie put in—"Tin yeers."

"What wages did you get at your last place?"

"Twinty—" I began.

"Twinty a week" ses Minnie boldly.

The lady looked tarribly startled. "Hoo did you wark for? Lit me see your riferinces" ses she.

Minnie hands her the boonch of papers shes after bringing along for me, and the lady looks at them throo her lorgon. Me own riference from Mrs. Wolley, which Miss Clare handed me proudly as I was stipping out, I also had handed to the lady, and I'm all oopset and red wid anger at the pinch on me arm Minnie is after giving me. The lady looks up wid her eyes frowning.

"Why these riferinces are for 2 differunt girls" ses she.

"Luk at that, wud yer?" ses Minnie, playfully. "Now didnt she after be giving you *my* riferences too by mishtake? *This* is mine" ses she, and tuk the letter frum Mrs. Wolley frum the lady's hand.

"Hoom." Ses the lady, and looks me over frum hed to foot throo her lorgon.

"Whats your name?" ses she, and refers to the letters.

"Delia" ses I innercently, "Miss Delia O'Malley if you plaze mam."

She set up stiff. Then she got up and putrified me wid a horty stare. Then she swipt over to Miss Flimflam, her silk pitticoat swishing behind her wid anger. Miss Flimflam cum over to me and grabbed me by the arm. She pushed me tord the stair.

"Minnie" ses I upstares, "its seeries throuble youve got me into now."

"Shaw!" ses Minnie, "Its dun ivery day. They no it. Delia theres twinty ladies for ivery wan girl. Your safe from anny blacklist darlint."

We seen Miss Flimflam cuming in at the door, and me gilty hart misgiving me, I grabbed Minnie by the arm and we wint out of wan dure as Miss Flimflam wint in by anuther.

"Delia, its a gump you are" ses Minnie with scorn, "but never mind, ye've dun enuff for to-day. We'll be back to-morrow."

V

Following Day

A woke. Arose again at 8:30. Dressed. Washed.

Minnie and I interfiewed the follering ladies in regard to a position.

Mrs. Spunk. She offered me $20 for cooking—2 in family. The wages were too small. I refused it wid contimt.

Mrs. Drool. $25. cook and londress. Minnie told her londry work wud spyle me hands.

Mrs. Lambkin—8 in family—Cooking. $30. Minnie sed Id be after waring the souls of me feet off rooning oop and down for the 8 of thim.

Mrs. Colebin: $30. Cooking and waiting on table. Minnie sed no cook cud be expicted to wate on table orlso. Me arms wud be after aking wid passing the hivvy dishes around.

Mrs. Sesick $40. Minnie sed we was above warking for sporting ladies at any price. Any lady, ses Minnie, who paints her hair and eyes and mouth and cheeks, and pads oop her natchurall hooman body isnt a lady at all, but a plane sporting woman.

VI

Two Weeks Later

I wint to the Alluyunce to-day for the first time alone. Minnie sed she was after being worn out wid kaping me frum accipting the woorthliss places offered by the pathrons of the Alluyunce. "Ye shud have enuff spunk yersilf by now" ses she. "Don't be saft. Raymimber ladies is your natrel inimies and beests of prey on poor hilpless sarvant girls."

Miss Flimflam spyed me as soon as I intered, and tuk me by the arm just as I was going to the room upstares.

"I'm glad" ses she corjully, "youve cum alone. Your frind was a inkubust" ses she. "Now cum rite along wid me. Theres a swate little lady wants a girl just like you" ses she, "and shes willing to pay you well and treet you" ses she, shmiling, "like a lady."

Wid that she leeds me acrost the room to wan of the sofies, and pushes out wid her foot wan of thim camp stules for the girls to sit upon.

"Good marning mam" ses I, lifting up me eyes modestly, and then I give sooch a joomp the dummed stool dubbles up under me and down I cum wid a boomp on the flure. For there sitting looking at me, very much surprysed and horty is Miss Claire hersilf. She smiled a bit whin I picked mesilf up, and ses I:

"Why, miss, the site of your pretty face just about flabbergasted me. How are you?" ses I.

"Quite well, thank you" ses she, very stiffly.

"And your mother?"

"—er mother is pretty well" ses she.

"Your father."

"Papa is—er—about the same" ses she.

"Mr. Johnny?"

"Still dy-et-ing, Delia."

"And Mr. James—"

"James—well, Delia, nun of us are very well. James *ses* he has intygischun."

"And what is that?" I inquires cooryissly

"—er—a sort of pane in the—er—stummick" ses she.

"Is it billy ake yure meening?"

She blushes, and ses:

"I suppose so."

"Who do be doing the cooking?" I arsks.

"Well—er—*I* tried. Delia don't you dare to larf" ses she indignantly.

"Larf!" ses I, "Why Lor bless your hart darlint, I'd more likely be weeping for the unhappy family."

She leened tords me, Wid her horchure quite gone, and looking as meek and swate as a kitten in thrubble.

"Delia" ses she, "Ive had elivin girls in since *you* left" ses she.

"You poor lamb!"

She puts on that weedling voyce she has whin bothering me to let her make mussy foodge in me frying pans:

"Delia" ses she, "w-wudnt you like to cum back?"

I shuk me hed. Then she set back, her horchure cuming back agin.

"O well" ses she, "theres hundreds of uther girls."

"Yes" ses I "the same as the elivin yourve had."

"Delia" ses she wid pashion "for pity sake do come back. I did thry to do my best but its like attempting to pleese a family of porkypines since you left and O! those awful craychures that came after you left. Why wan of thim" ses she indignantly "was want to tak the soyled table linen—aven the lace doylies—for dish cloths."

"My God! miss" ses I "you don't meen them buties you made yersilf?"

"Yes indade," ses she turning her face away.

"Miss Claire" ses I.

"Yes Delia" ses she quickly, turning round in a bounce.

"Nothing" ses I, angry wid mesilf for me meekness.

"*Delia*" ses she despritly, "we've tuk a place in the cuntry. We *must* have a girl. Its dredful to think of being widout one. O Delia, *do please* cum wid us."

"No-o—Miss—" ses I a bit tremendulussly.

"I'll—I'll—give you that old—er—its not relly old—black taffita jacket of mine" ses she.

I skuk me hed.

"—and the skurt wid the box plates" ses she "and you can have that tucked shemysett—you no, the one you do up so luvly."

"No Miss Claire" ses I firmly, getting up. "I'm for uther wark than gineral housework." She got up also, and her voyce sounds a bit shakey.

"Very well Delia" ses she. "Its hard on me—so much trubble—"
Thin her blue eyes run over, and she walked away, wiping thim wid her
handkychiff. I seen her go out the dure. I filt a sinking at me hart. Minnie
Carnavan was forgotten, and like the gump she ses I am I made a grand
dash fur the dure, wid all the Miss Flimflams of the Alluyunce, and the
ladies thimsilves gaping after me in horrow. I seen Miss Claire half a
block away, and I run after her puffing:

"Miss Claire! Darlint! Miss Claire!" I called after her. She turned
about and guve me wan look. Then she made a like grand dash as mesilf.
Her parrysol flew out of her hand, also her rist bag.

"O Delia—you *duck*" ses she, and kissed me wid a smack, hugging
and squazing me manewile.

There cum three yung doods marching down the Avenoo, and as
Miss Claire taks me in her arms the bauld yung chaps stud still and
looked at us and shmiled. Thin one bint down and keerfully picked up
the parrysol and wiped it wid the sleeve of his foine gray coat. As me
and Miss Claire extrycate ourselves he offers it to her wid a bow. She
toorned red as a peeney and her bloo eyes guv one luk up at the dood,
then drapped demoorly:

"Thanks" ses she, "Thanks agin" ses she, as he likewise returns her
rist-bag. He lifted up his hat, waited a bit for more thanks, and thin
marched aff, shmiling like his face wud bust. *She* smiles too, and ses I,
boorsting:

"A roomance, Miss Claire! Be all the saints in hivin and airth, ye've
luked into the eyes of your hoosband."

"Nonsense" ses she, laffing, "you're the same old silly sintimental
Delia. Cum home deer."

VII

Two Weeks Later

A woke, aroze, washed, dressed, made me bed. Spint the bitter part of a our or more trying to make that dummed stove burn. Its a wild wilderniss of a place is this and its hard indade for a pure loansum innercent female to bare the silence of the atmust-fear. Whin Miss Claire a spoke of the country I had thort of Asbry Park or Coney Island and such like sinsible places, but indade theres no bordwalk here at all at all and the only kinds of bands and orkistrys is in the trees. Wirra, wirra, wirra! The kitchens in the bastement and the dining-room a flure above. I shuk me hed over this contrivance whin I first seen it, but Miss Claire ses very swately:

"Now doant you be arfter wurrying about that" ses she "fur theres a dumm waiter in the butlers pantry."

Wid that she showed me a contrapshon in the wall, and wint to work pulling at the ropes.

"Dumm!" ses I, shouting wid me rarth, "Is it dumm you call the dumm thing. My God, Miss," ses I "Its noysy enuff to waken the deff."

"Nites enuff" ses I me milincoly hivvy on me chist, "it'll be all nites now for me Miss Claire."

"You Goose!" ses she, "I don't meen *that* kind of Nite, but—but— you know—a grate handsome fellar of a Nite" ses she.

"Is it a *bow* ye're maning?" I arsks sarcarskullully.

"Yes Delia dear."

"And sorrer a Nite of that kind will I get Miss" ses I moanfully.

She opened her blue eyes big, and shuk her hed mysteerissly.

"Its in the cuntry they abownd" ses she.

"And lit them cum abownding" ses I snorting, "Its a foine gintlemanly sort" ses I "wud abound into the prisince of a loidy. If it's oanly the bounding kind ye're haveing here, Miss Claire, theyd bitter kape their distance frum me kitchen."

VIII

A Few Days Later

Awoke—aroze—washed—dressed—made me bed—Imtied me slops.

I tuk a bit of paper from Mr. John's desk, and I penned the follering warning in plane litters and langwidge:

Brikfust Sarved
At 8 Oanley
No Brikfust
Sarved Later

This I taxed artiskully upon the dining-room door—facing all eyes.

Mr. John—ating his loan cup of hot water looks up. Hes a gintle spaking gintleman in contrarst to his bruther James. The rayson of this Mr. Wolley explayned to me wanse was that Mr. John is an eediotor wile Mr. James is a bawld voiced orthor, spaking, ses Mr. Wolley, wid the orful tung of the muck raker. Well Mr. John looks up gintly and fidgets his paper and ses mildly:

"Er—Delia—er—"

"Well?" ses I, fite in me toans.

"Another cup of hot water if you plase" ses he.

He hild up the cup befure his eyes suspishussly.

"—er Delia" ses he, making an effet to mollyfy me timper. "How do you like it here" ses he.

"Like it! My God its a loan wilderniss of a place, sor," ses I.

"Shaw!" ses he, "Why theeres forty-two families on the Poynt."

"The Poynt?"

"Yes. They call this neck of land the Poynt" ses he "I suppose becorse its just a poynt of land running into the Sound."

"Its a bloont poynt" ses I.

"It is" ses he, "but down at the ind of it, there *is* a very fine poynt of land. Me brother waggushly corls it 'Rogues Poynt'" ses he.

"And why sor?"

"Haw, haw!" ses he, larfing into his napkin.

Mr. James cum sontering in joost thin in tinnis pants. He tramped acrost me imacklate floor, banged out a chare and doomped himself into it.

"Me brikfust in a hurry Delia" ses he. "Whats the joke Johnny" ses he to his larfing brother.

"I was telling Delia the name ye've given the Poynt—Rogues Poynt."

"Hum!" ses Mr. James, ating amorosly on a grape froot. "Its like this Delia" ses he, guving me a seeriess look, "The 2 show places on the ind of the Poynt are occipied respictably by an Oil magnut and a Insurince Prissydint."

"And be they rogues?" asks I innercently.

"Dammed raskils" ses Mr. James sollemly.

IX

Another Day

A roze. Got up. Dressed. Made me bed. Imtied me slops.
"I want you all to lissen to me" ses Miss Claire, adrissing the assimbled family in the dining-room. "Now" ses she, "if I'm to be housekaper and we cant afford but wan girl and the works altogether too hevvy for Delia alone and shell be laving us if—"

"Sh!" says her mother, "spake lower. Shes in the bootlers pantry, making the salad.

"Nonsinse" ses Mr. James, "shes at the keyhole lissening."

"Well, but do lissen all," airges Miss Claire. "Iverybody" ses she, "has got to do his indivijool share of work. The lons must be cut. A garden must be planted. Frish vigetables are absolootely nicissiry. James" ses she swately, "*You* can cut the lons."

"Lons!" cryes he in thoondering toans. "I cut lons! Why me deer sister its aginst me most artistick instink" ses he. "Its wan of me firm and uncontradictible opinyons that lons shud remane uncut. Why annyone can have *cut* lons. Luk at the places around us, widout an ixcipshun the lons are cut slick and smooth as a yooths chin. I tell you sister mine" ses he "its more artistick to let your grass grow long."

"Nonsinse" ses Miss Claire.

Here Mr. John tuk up the coodgills for his sister.

"Unkemp lons" ses he, "are artistick on the same principle as the ass is a boheemyun who smoaks and drinks in out of way outlandish joynts and has an inborn prejydiss aginst a manicar parlor. 'Dirty nales' ses he, in the like toan of me brother 'is artistick.' Jimmy, boy, explane the artistick sinse of uncut lons?"

"Deny it if you can" shouted Mr. James, thoomping on the table "I challinge you. Do you mane to assert that the fat broaker who kapes his lons and drives clane as a well swipt parlor has the same artistick sinse as the chap who lets his grarss grow gracefully aloft kissing the gintle seffers which swape the jewey—"

Here I heard the contemshus russel of Mr. John's paper.

"Do be sinsible Jimmy" ses Mrs. Wolley. "Claire is quite right. The lons must be cut. If we don't cut them nobody'll call on us. We'll be marked and shunned in this community."

Here both Mr. James and John assayed to spake at wanse, the latter aisily being drowned out by the thoonder toans of the hedstrung orthor.

"Mother!" ses he "I'm ashamed of you. Can I beleeve me eers. Is it me own mother—the woman who gave me berth spaking? Do you achooly mane that you are inspired wid a dred that these essenshilly vulger fatheaded raskilly rich nayburs of ours may not call on us? What!" ses he, drowning the interrupting voyce of Mr. John, "Do you *desire* there acquaytinse?"

"Me brotyer" ses Mr. John gintly, "finds his vocatshun rooning from his finger tips to his tung. To him the mere fack of being rich is to be likewise a fool and nave."

"I claim" ses Mr. James thoomping on the table "that a man cannot make a billion onestly. I agree wid me frind Andrew Carnegie, who denies he sed it, that its impossible."

"What of those who inherit?" ses Mrs. Wolley.

"Poony-soled, puppy heded eediots. What rite I asks have they to *kape* the money stolen from the peeple by there fathers?"

Mr. Wolley put in a word here edgewise.

"It seems to me James" ses he "that you are wilfully departing from the mooted subject. I belave in dyagression—to a limited extint—and whin by gintle degrees it permits us to cum back to the subjeck under discushion."

"Yes" ses Miss Claire, "we must get back to the lons. Its settled. James you will cut them at leest wanse a week."

"Once a week! Lord God of Isreel!" grones Mr. James, "I'll be a fissicle reck befure the summer wanes."

"Next" ses Miss Claire, "Johnny *you* must take care of the horse."

I thort Mr. John must be tearing up his paper, from the noyse of its russeling. I pressed up closer to the dure.

"Claire, my deer" ses he, "I beg you think befure you spake. I've never handled a horse in me life. If you contimplate the purchase of a baste, you will have to hire a man to care for it. I draw" ses he "the lines at stable work."

"Very well" ses she, "*you* can go walk the mile or 2 to the village after the mail."

"We'll take turn about" ses Mr. John.

"What!" shouts Mr. James, "and me wid my grass cutting!"

"To orffset that" ses Miss Claire, "John can rayse our vigitables."

"My deer child—" began Mr. John "I know not the first thing of—er—"

"You're all just horrid." ses Miss Claire and she pushed back her chare. "Very well then, I wash my hands of the hole affare."

"James" ses Mr. Wolley in sturn commanding toans, "You will cut the lons as intercated by your sister. John" ses he "I will expect you to rayse addecut vigitables for the table."

"Daddy" ses Miss Claire, "*you'll* go to the Post-Office wont you like an angel?"

"Certainly my deer" ses he, "It will give me grate pleshure." A silence followed here, and the auld gintleman must have bethort him of his hasty promise, for ses he:

"We will kape a horse" ses he, "at a neerby livery stable."

Mr. James bust out larfing.

"Whats my juties to be?" swately inquires Mrs. Wolley, trying to change the paneful subject.

"Oh mamma" ses Miss Claire, "*you* may care for the chickens."

"Let me see" ses Mrs. Wolley "Aren't there such things as—er—lice—connected with chickens?"

"Yes deer—but if you'll kape the coop always witewashed" ses Miss Claire, "the lice'll go."

Mrs. Wolley coffed unaisily.

"And now *you*, miss?" shouts Mr. James, "what have you left for yourself to do?"

"Theres a thousand and wan things, but as my cheef and spechul jooty outside of the hivvy housekaping wid the constant tack and diplomassy it intales to kape our unsertin Delia, I will undertake to—er—rayse sweet *flowers* for the beutifying of our lons and house."

"Call *that* work!" larfs Mr. James.

"You inappreeshitive duffer" ses Mr. John in his gintlest voyce. "I vote that we adjoin."

"One moment" ses Mr. James. "What of Billy? Is he to be the sole mimber of this innergitick family to live in aise and lazy cumfut?"

"No indeedy" ses Miss Claire. "Never! Tho but 6 yeers of age, hes old enuff to ern his daily bred. Willy" ses she "shall be our yuniversul caddy. His will be the tax of carrying water to the hungry thoorsty wans what toyle."

X

THE NEXT DAY

I was up to me eers in work—it being wash day. As I carried the clothes out to be hung I noted the following: Mr. John was walking up and down taking triminjus long stips back and forth over the back lon. Wid the tales of his coat flying out behind him and his spickticles hanging by a string from his eer he looked so like a loonytick that I drapped me baskit of clothes.

"My God, Mr. John" I exclaimed involuntarararily "Are you sun struck. Whats the trubble" ses I, and I stopped him in his mad careerer as Mr. James wud call it by grabbing him by his cote tales. He turned about, looks at me wid wild eyes and ses horsely:

"Twinty-two and a harf—twinty-two and a—Bother the girl!" ses he interrupting himsilf, "Are you crazy? Let go me cote tales." I releesed him. Ses he irrytibly:

"Can't you see I'm bizzy? I'm meshuring off me vigitible garden" and wid that he starts marching over the same line agin.

"My God, Mr. John!" ses I "are you using yur legs for a meshure?"

But he herd me not. I toar me horryfied eyes away frum the madman, and just then I seen Mr. James. He was standing also on the lon, neerer the frunt of the house. He's leening on the lon mower, and if ever I seen dispare in human eyes it was in those orbs of Mr. James. I wint to him wid me hart full of sympathy for the lad.

"Whats ailing you Mr. James?" I arsks.

"The lons!" ses he. "You will obsarve Delia, that I'm commincing me tax at the beginning of the week, for I am firmly convinsed no human arm cood cut those lons in less than sivin days."

"Why don't you get a dago, Mr. James" ses I.

"Sh!" ses Mr. James, guving me arm a shuv. "Spake lowly Delia. Obsarve" and he poynted acrost the lons.

There aginst the finse which divides our place from a grate estate was Miss Claire hersilf *digging*. She had a little red gingum aprun over her dress and the slaves was rolled oop to the ilbos. On her hed was the strangest looking site of a hat. I reckynised it wid horrer. It wuz a Spanish monsterosity Mr. James brot back wid him that time he wint to

Pannyma to expose the Prissydint. Until this day Miss Claire had yused it for a waste paper barsket in her room, tying it in a boonch wid ribbon and hanging it artisticully upon the wall. Now she woar it on her hed! Joost thin she looked up from her digging and seen me.

"Now Delia" ses she "don't be bothering Jimmy. Hes got lots to do. We *all* have" she adds swately.

"What be you doing Miss Claire?" arsks I, going over to her, and looking wid suspisshon at the hole she's after diggin. "My God Miss" ses I "it looks like a grave."

"Delia! Why" ses she "I'm sitting out a flouring hidge. I'm follring the rules of the bist orthorities on hortyculcheer. See:" and she poynted to her pockets which were boolging out wid books. "All are agreed" ses she "that a gardin shud be begun wid a flouring hidge. My gardin will be one glow of luvliness from spring till frorst and maybe later. Its possible."

"But miss" ses I "ye'll nade a gardiner for the tax"

"Never! Why I've been setting up nites studying me subjeck. I expect to devoat—" just thin she guv a little joomp and her cheeks turned pink wid excitemint.

"My goodness Delia!" ses she wispering, "th-theres *a* man" ses she.

"Whare?" ses I, glaring about me, riddy for war upon anny dirty tramps trispessing upon our place.

"The other side the fince" ses she, wispering. I looked over, but seen no wan.

"Are you quite *sure*?" asks she, trimbling a bit.

"I am" ses I. She turned pale, and siesed hold of me arm.

"Delia!" ses she whispering "d-d-d-do you remimber that—that—young man who—"

"Is it your future hoosband ye're maning?"

"Nonsinse" ses she blushing, "but—but I meen him anyhow. Well—well—do you know—I—I—I'm afrade he's *honting* me" ses she.

"My God miss" ses I "do you think he's a banshee?"

"No, no Delia—but—but well" ses she, "the fack is I'm always *thinking* about him, and now—now ackshully I thort I saw him—over there" ses she.

"Suppose" ses I "you tak a look again Miss Claire."

"I cant" ses she, shinking aginst me, "and beside the finse is so high. Its—its—much taller than I am" ses she.

"Ah come on" ses I, and pulled her to the finse. "Here miss, I'll lift you up," and wid that I grabbed her by the waste and hawled her up. She screemed. I dropped her wid a boomp, for there looking over, rubbing his hed where Miss Claire has boomped aginst it, is the Madison Avenoo dood. Miss Claire tuk to her feet and wint flying tord the house, her books drapping out of her pockits as she run.

XI

NEXT DAY

Larst nite Miss Claire cum into me bedroom. She looked like a bit of a girl in her little frilled nitedress and her pretty hare hanging down her back in 2 curly brades. "Are you awake?" ses she turning on the lite. "Don't be angry please Delia deer" ses she. "I wanted to talk to somewan."

She coodled oop aginst me, thin she laned over and whispered:

"Delia, tell me the trooth, d-d-did you see him—k-kiss me?" ses she flushing all over.

"The yung spalpeen!" ses I, and thin she hid her face in her hand.

"Oh Delia I'm—I'm—so—*ashamed* I d-don't know *what* to do."

"Do!" ses I. "Why tell your brothers darlint. They'll swape the airth wid the impidint yung spalpeen."

"No, no, no! We must never breethe a word" ses she. "Promise me you wont, Delia," and she sarches me face.

"Darlint" ses I "all the torchures of the dummed could not unlock me lips. Your sacred swatehart is secure in me bussum."

Wid that she guv me a kiss, and wint steeling out agin.

"Mr. John" ses I, this marning while hes ating his loan brikfust (a cup of biling water) I'm looking for sartin infamation.

"Well fire away Delia" ses he still absarbed in his paper.

"If a lady" ses I "was to kiss a gintleman wid hoom she was not acquinted wud the gintleman be insoolted?"

He put down his paper, tuk off his glarses and looked at me sollemly.

"Has some wan kissed *you* Delia?" ses he.

"My God, no sir" ses I, "but I'm studying the respectful sects."

He retired behind his paper agin, and Mr. James cum wistling into the room. Hes very cheerful these days is Mr. Jimmy. He gets app, he ses, at 5 A.M. in the morning to cut the lons. The tax he ses at that wiching our is anchanting. Ivery marning when we get up we see a porshon of the lon cut. At 8 Mr. James sonters in frish from his after cutting lon bath as he calls it. "Sum day" ses Mr. John who has his trubbles digging up the airth where the vigitibles are to go "I'll try your skeem."

"Don't" ses Mr. James anxshissly. "What applies to lons may not do for gardins."

Well this marning, Mr. John repeats me quistion to his brother.

"Delia" ses he "wants to know how a man wud feel if suddintly assolted and amberaced by a yung and pretty lady—of coorse shes yung and pretty, Delia eh?" ses he.

"What wud he do!" ses Mr. James. "Lord God of Isreel why he'd—he'd pursoo her like a caveman till she guv anuther kiss."

"My God!" ses I drapping the dishes in me hand, "and wimmen is jest alike."

I wint down to me kitchen, whare I guv a peece of me mind to the grocer's man. Shure he do be after charging the Wolleys the most oonherd of prices for the food, and whin I'm after making a complaint in the madam's name, the raskill opp and offers me a boniss.

"And what is that?" ses I.

"Tin per sint" ses he. "Its the custom on the Poynt amang the cooks to accipt a boniss fram the tradesmen. We tak it out of the peeple thimsilves" ses he, "eyther in wate or price."

"Is it a thafe ye'd mak me?" ses I, faulding me arms over me chist. "thin ye may thank yere stars" ses I "that Miss Claire is too angaged to be interrupted at the prisint moment, for its she hersilf wud be showing you the dure. As it is I take the tax upon mesilf."

Wid that I saysed hauld of the broom, and drove the craychure out. I seen Miss Claire joomp oop from whare shes digging at her floury hidge, and as the thafe wint flying down the parth, wid me at his heels, both she and the dood bust out larfing, she thrying her bist to kape a strate face.

XII

A Week Later

O rtermobiles" ses Mr. Wolley tying his horse up feercely to the veranda post "is a meniss to our prisint civilisashun. Nowadays" ses he, "its impossible for a gintleman to drive in quite peece in aven the most seclooded porshun of the woods. The gratest evil which these damnible veehicles have brot" ses he "is its maleevilint effect upon the conshunse and disposition of modun peeble. Peeple who own these infernul evil smelling noysy cursed cars are like the victims of some orful drug—devoyed of dacinsy—of rispict—of consideration and proper mercy tord there feller beings. There shud be a lor passed making it a criminal offinse punishible by the pinnytensherry to ride the dammed masheen on the public hyways at all. Rodes and highways are the legitimut proppety of horses and pedestryians. Its a disgrace to our modun civilysashun that we have cum to such a sorry pass—a week-need trimbling fritened lot afrade to vinchure forth for feer of having our lives cut aff widout warning by these infernal veehicles."

Wid that he mops his brow, and sets down widout looking on the shteps. I was swaping down the verandahs wid a pale of water, and had driven the family at the poynt of me broom to the lons below. Whin the auld gintleman found himself sated in a pool of the water he shoots up wid a yell. Miss Claire runs forward and trys to squaze the water out from his cote tales—larfing as her father swares.

"Poor old daddy!" ses she "I'm afrade if I let you go arfter the male much longer you'll be a pray to nerviss prosperation."

"Do you imagine" ses the auld gintleman feercely "that I'm to be robbed of me daily drive by a parcel of godless hairbrained—damnible—"

"Papa" ses little Billy, bringing over his pale from his sandpile. "*I* loves the oretermobiles?"

"Why bless me hart!" ses the auld man melting "and what do you know of them you raskill" ses he.

"I had a ride in one yistiday" ses Billy.

"What!" ses the hole family at wance.

"Yes" ses Billy, nodding his little hed, "Theres a grate big wan in that place there" ses he poynting, "and yistiday when Claire was digging her old flours there cum a yung man who luked over the fince, and he sed—he sed—"

Miss Claire wint first crimson thin wite. Then crimson agin.

"Billy deerie" ses she, "cum and let me swing you in the hammick."

"Go on Billy" airges Mr. James, guving his sister a quare look.

"He sed good morning to Claire, and she was very rood and jest wint on wid her digging and then he sed he was sorry and he cudent help himself becoz he herd what she sed about honting her, and then he seen me and said hello yung wan, come over here, and then I went and he reeched down and lifted me up and tuk me over to his place. And he guv me a ride in his nortemobile and on a donkey's back, did'nt he Claire?"

She sed, widout looking up.

"I suppose he did, Billy, but I" ses she "was too bizzy. I—I d-didnt look" ses she.

Mr. James bounces up. "Claire" ses he "that hidge of yours is taking a jolly long time to dig."

Mrs. Wolley looked turribly alarmed.

"He was probably sum gardiner or groom" ses she "Did you spake to him Claire deer?"

"*No!*" ses Miss Claire wid emfasis.

"Yet you let him take little Billy?" ses Mr. James.

"Am I me brother's kaper?" ses she flushing round on thim all.

"I won't have Claire badgered" ses the auld gintleman. "Is she rayspunsible for the silly thricks of the yung ass in there? He's the very one who whin I refoosed to move out of the rode to let his infernal masheen go by drove it rite under me horse's nose, almost upsetting me. Billy" ses he, "if I heer of your taking any more rides or spaking to the man over there I'll whip you. You under stand sir?"

"Yessir" whimpered the preshus lamb and flew to me arms for comfut.

XIII

Another Day

Are you bizzy, Delia" arsks Mr. John, cumming into me kitchen wid a barskit.

"I'm oop to me eers sor" ses I. I wus setting on the ice crame freezer, thrying to cool aff, after making the crame for loonch.

"Wud you like to make sum monney" ses he.

"Shure darlint" ses I.

"I'm tired of this gardin bisiness," ses he. "Now these are seeds." He set the barskit down befure me. "Theyve joost arrived. Heres a book giving fool instruckshuns how to plant thim. You go ahed," ses he "and plant thim whin you git a chance. I'd suggest" ses he "that you do it in the airly marning, but me brother James who cuts the lons at those unairthly ours wud see you, so do it whenever the feeld is cleer. And heres a dollar."

"Thank you sor" ses I. I set to wark at wance imtying the seeds from there respictible packages into me bred pan. Then I give them all a good mixup thegither. The book I shuved aside wid scorn.

"Anny wan I'm thinking but a doom eediot cud plant seeds in the grownd" ses I to mesilf, "and what wud I be arfter needing instroockshuns for?"

Joost thin Miss Claire cum in to guv me the orders os I tuk it for the day. Shes a bit flustered and oopset.

"O Delia" ses she "what *do* you think. A cupple of papa's frinds have cum up frum town, and we'll have to kape thim for loonch. What have we got?"

"See for yersilf" ses I, biling over wid rage. Company indade on Winsdy, wid the tale ind of the ironing to finish, and seeds to be planted in the gardin.

"O deer!" ses she "there is'nt a thing hardly. What will we do? I'm sure none of those trade people will deliver in time. What did you plan to give us to-day Delia?"

"Its *hash* ye'll get and be thankful" ses I.

"But theres no cold meat aven" ses she in disthress.

"I'll attind to that" ses I.

"But—"

"Now see here Miss Claire, its no time I have for argying wid me hands boorsting wid wark this morning. Will you be going or shull I?"

"Well Delia deer" ses she meekly, "If you *can* make aven hash out of—nothing—c-cudent you just cuvver it over wid mashed pertaters and brown it in the uvven? It tastes diffruntly that way."

"I'll see about it" ses I.

"O Delia!" ses Miss Claire, "be nice or I don't see how I'll dare to ask a speshul favour of you."

"Favour is it?" ses I toorning upon her. She roon ap to me, and befure I can shpake anuther word, shes got her arms about me.

"Now lissen deer" ses she. "I've finished me floury hidge and this afternoon I must shtart on the beds. *You* do the digging for me like an angel" ses she.

"Digging is it? Do you tak me for—"

"Please, please" ses she.

"It depinds intirely on how the loonch goes" ses I gruffly. "Now raymimber not wan ward of crittersickem will I be heering to."

"Not wan word" ses she.

After she had gone I dischuvvered that there was'nt a speck of tea in the house and exactly three coffee beens oanly. I wint upshstairs speshully to infarm Miss Claire. "Be careful now" ses I "to ignoar the subject. Lit your gests think ye've forgotten the biverage."

All wint well for loonch, till Mr. James, soospecting the thruth, ondertook to refer to me hash as "patty de 4 grass a la Delia" a dish ses he of our Delia's own invinshun. I guv wan look at Miss Claire, and she changed the subject. Thin Mrs. Wolley asked the lady which she wud have—coffee or tee, and before the unforchnit craychure cud answer I spoke up at wance:

"Ye'll get neyther" ses I.

Miss Claire at wance requested me to bring on sum more "snow hash." Wid that me last bit of payshunce wint, for theres not anuther speck of the stuff to be had.

"Do ye think" ses I "that wan can of potted ham will feed a large family to more than wan sarve a peece?"

"Potted ham!" ses Mr. James, forgitting himself and the company.

"Potted ham!" ses I, "for its no meet in the house at all we're after having, and shure the potted stuff is good enuff for you." Wid that I wint into the pantry and got the can and tuk it into the dining-room and showed it to the silent family.

"Is it misdoubting me word ye are" ses I. "Then see for yersilves." And I showed them the can wid its pretty ligind: "Guvvymint inspeckshun."

Mr. James got up and left the room. Mr. Wolley, groonting followed. "Excuse me!" ses I and walked out also.

Felling a bit sorry for the unforchnit family I got riddy a foine dinner, and was after rolling me pie paste when Miss Claire cum in and coxed me into going wid her to the gardin. She put me to wark digging a hole in the cinter of the illygunt lon, frish cut by Mr. James. "The boys have gone bathing" ses she, "papa's out driving and mama's aslape. Nows our chance. O Delia how forchnit it is our gests didn't stay for dinner too."

Thin she left me, and wint over to her floury hidge, whare she neels down and looks at the airth. All of a sudden she guv a little cry:

"Cum quick Delia!" Ses she "Cum quick."

I rooshed over wid me ho, thinking theres a snake or tode in the grass.

"Look!" ses Miss Claire, trimbling wid excitement.

"What! Where is the craychure?"

"There! See, its me hedge!" ses she. "O Delia its the first showing. In a little wile it'll grow bigger and bigger, and by and by therell be flours—beauties. And I" ses she "did it all mesilf—wid these hands. Don't you see it—that little speck of grane."

"Sorrer a bit do I see darlint" ses I.

"Why Delia! Its there oonless me eyes decave me."

"They don't" ses a bold voice boldly, and the dood nixt door lanes over the fince and stares sintimintully at the spot where Miss Claire is poynting. She guv a little start and blushed. Then she arsks sarcarskully:

"May I arsk if you can see it at that distunce?"

"Certainly" ses he at wunce, "but I belave I cud see it better if I cam a little nearer." Wid that he joomps over the fince and walks to where Miss Claire is neeling. Together they look at the airth.

"Bully for you!" ses he offering to shake the hand which she holds back timidly. "Why" ses he "its—its a—a rose, is'nt it?" ses he.

"No" ses Miss Claire withdroring the hand she had joost surrindered. "Its a hullyhock" ses she.

"Well its fine anyhow" ses he, looking at her wid both his eyes popping out of his hed. "Youre quite a horty culchurist" ses he.

"O no indade" ses she, "its me first attimp. Do you" ses she "know anything about it?"

"Well" ses he "I can tell a vylet from a rose and a dandylion from a daysy."

"Then" ses she, "you wont be intrested in my little gardin."

"Wont I" ses he, so vylently she drops her eyes. "Why I'm ackshully captifated by that little speck of green" ses he. "Aren't you its creator?"

"Wate till it begins to bloom" ses she enthoosicully. Joost thin she seen her brothers coming in wid the bote oars on their shoulders. She started away from the dood, and wint narvissly to meet thim. The dood histated a moment, and then wint ap to the boys. He hild out his hand.

"I'm your next dure naybor" ses he "and I drapped over to make a corl."

"How do" ses Mr. James giving him a corjul shake "Pretty good bathing here" ses he "Ever go out?"

"O yes" ses the dood "We have a little privit beech of our own. Your welcom to use it any time."

Mr. James frowned.

"The public beech is good enuff" ses he shortly, but Mr. John ses at wance:

"Thank you I'll thry your place sum day."

XIV

ANOTHER DAY

James" ses Mr. Wolley coming into brikfust at an oonexpected airly our "you're a frord and raskill sir" ses he.

The family all looked startled.

"Yes sir" ses his father sturnly "ye've been deceiving your sister shamefully. You have been practicing a frord. I happened" ses he turning to the rist of the family "to awaken airly this marning and going to the window to pull down the shade I saw a man ingaged in cutting the lons. Congrachulating mesilf on the possession of such an industryiss and paynestaking sun, I corled to the fellow, who thereupon looked up. He was a sworthy faced working man—an Italyun. There Claire" ses he "is the sacred of your brothers well cut lons."

"Jimmy!" ses Miss Claire reproachfully.

He puts his hands into his pants pocket and thrys to look indiffrunt.

"I ordered the feller off the grounds" continued her father "for I was determined that no sun of mine shud shirk his respunsibilities in that shameliss fashun. Sir" ses he, turning upon Mr. James, "you'll be good enuff to resoom the cutting of the lons after brikfust."

For wance Mr. James was silent. He et his brikfust widout opening his mouth wance.

XV

ANOTHER DAY

A little widder who lives across the rode cum to-day to call upon the family. She brung along wid her a yung thing swate enuff to ate. They cum driving up behind a pare of spanking horses and drov up under the port coshare. Mr. James was cutting his milincoly lon, and he niver looked up at all.

The younger one called to him swately.

"Will you hold the horses, plase."

Mr. James pushed back his hat and glared like he wad bite her.

"I beg your pardin" ses she and the widder begins to larf and closed up her parrysol. Joost then Mr. John cum round from the back of the house. He lucks very straynge and funny, being in overalls, his spicticles poysed on the tip of his nose, his hair standing opp where his fingers have been running through it. Its a turrible tax the poor gintleman has been doing. Shure hes been all day digging up the seeds which I carefully mixed and planted. The ladies in the carriage try to stop larfing and the yunger one joomps out.

"Is Mrs. Wolley at home" ses she.

Miss Claire laves her floury hidge and dood, and wint running forward, wid her little muddy hands hild out. I seesed hauld of an aprun on the line and tied it on me. Thin I wint to anser the dure. Miss Claire is leeding them on to the veranda.

"I'm Miss Wolley" ses she, "you find us all ingaged at our respictuf toyle. My brother James cuts the grass, John's the vigitable gardiner, and I rayse swate flours—"

"What fun!" ses the widder clasping her hands, "How perfeckly deliteful. It mus be just like playing, is'nt it," and she turned her big black eyes on Mr. John.

"Will ye walk inside" ses I, braking in here, "Mrs. Wolley will be down in a moment. Shes not well, but she's for seeing you. Joost have a seet, she ses."

"O lets sit out here!" ses the widder. "You were talking of your gardin?" ses she turning to Mr. John wid a smile.

"—er yes" ses he. "But I'm a mere noviss. Do you understand anything about the art?"

"Do I?" ses she, sitting in the saftest veranda chare, "Why I've a reppytashun in the Poynt for me vigitibles. Have'nt I Una?" and she appealed to her frind, who has just infarmed Mr. James that sumtimes she cuts her papa's lons wid her own fare hands, jest for exsysise.

"Yes" ses Miss Una, nodding her pretty hed, "Why" ses she "theres a sertin kind of turnip nown to fame as The Widdy Jane."

"Una!" ses the widder larfing, "but relly" ses she turning back to Mr. John agin "I manage my own little farm all mesilf."

I let Mrs. Wolley out thru the fly dure and thin the auld gintleman wint out, also wid his face red and shining from the quick shave he's given it. They all torked and larfed and thin finully got up to go. Thin Miss Claire asks carelessly.

"And hoo are our naybours on this side?" and she intercated the doods place.

"Have'nt they called on you yet" arsks the widder.

Mrs. Wolley frowned a bit, but Miss Claire ses swately:

"Oh yes one of the suns called."

"One of the suns!" ses the widder, "Why Harry's the only child. Una here," ses she, smiling "can tell you all about him."

"I!" ses Miss Una, opening her brown eyes wide, "O yes" ses she "Harry and I yused to be sweet on aich other senturies ago. Hes a deer boy" ses she, "and you'll meet his mother soon I suppose, and old S. Judd Dudley."

Mr. Wolley and Mr. James both bounced up in their seets. The auld gintleman conthrolled himsilf.

"Pardon me, my deer" ses he "but did I oonderstand you to say our naybour's name was Dudley—S. Judd Dudley?"

"Yes" ses she "the famiss S. Judd. Youve herd of him of coorse."

"I have" ses Mr. Wolley slowly, and the hole family looked at aich uther strayngely.

XVI

A Week Later

"The curse of true love" ses Miss Claire mornfully "never did run smoothly. O Delia" ses she "I wish I were ded!"

"Whats the thrubble, darlint?" ses I stopping me wark for a moment.

"Don't you know?" she arsks.

"Why no darling. Do you think I'm at the kayhole *all* the time?"

She larfed a bit throo her teers. Then she set down, and put her chin on her little hand.

"Delia" ses she "do you know I havent spoken to Mr. Dudley for a week."

"My God miss" ses I, "are you cutting the lad?"

She nods her hed sadly.

"The poor lad!" ses I "and he do be wayting for you ivery day at the floury hidge."

"Papa wont let me go neer it" ses she wid a sob.

"Then why dussent the yung spalpeen cum to the house thin?" ses I indigantly.

"He did" ses she "twice—and—and James insoolted him. O Delia" ses she, and hides her face in her hands.

I drors her into me arms and pets her like a babby, while she poars out into me sympatetic eers her thrubbles.

"You know Delia" ses she "papa yused to be professer of mathymatucks at Logun Yunyversity. Well last winter James began that orful muck rake riting. It seems Mr. Dudley had given a grate many chares to Logun Yunyversity."

"Chares darlint? For the lads to set upon?"

"No Delia—but it dussent matter. Anyhow he was a grate power in papa's colluge. Well James began exposing millynairs in the magazines and papers and by and by rote a powerful artuckle on tinted munney. He sed orful things of Mr. Dudley who wint clane crazy about it. You see he loved to pose as a bennyfactory to his cuntry and James had shown him as he was. It wassent papa's folt but Mr. Dudley revinged himself on papa. He got the thrustees to ask for papa's assignashun and now papa joins with James in thinking him the gratest rarscal of the time. So you can see Delia" ses she, her lips trimbling "that nachully they hafnt much yuse for Harry, and—and they've forbidden me to speak to him again."

"You poor lamb" ses I "but shure if I was Mr. Harry I'd find a way to see you if I had to sneek into the kitchen itself to do it."

"Delia!" ses she, clutching me arm excitedly, "What an idear! Oh Delia" ses she "Why not?"

XVII

ANOTHER DAY

Wrote a letter to-day to me frind Minnie Carnavan asking her advise. It were as follows:

Deer Minnie

I hope you are well as this laves me at prisint. Its a long time since I seen yer swate face, but wid the wark of a family of six to do, besides helping Mr. James to cut the lons, Mr. John to plant the gardin, whitewashing of the chicken coop for Mrs. Wolley, I'm clane doon up whin nite cums. But theres anuther kind of wark I'm lately doing, and being its what mite be called mind wark me nerves ar beginning to thrubble me and whin annyone spakes to me at all I shtart upp like a thafe cort at a crime. Its minny a day since I wint to confesshun and me mind is deeply thrubbled wid the thort that the praste will refuse me absilooshun.

The thruth of the matter be that I'm helping a dorter decave her luving parents. Its 2 weeks now since I begun to let Mr. Harry in at the back dure. Me foine privit dining-room which Miss Claire had told me was for me to sit in alone is occupied in the avening excloosively by Miss Claire and her bow. To add to me minny kares the child requires me to chappyrong her as shes after calling it. And so ivry nite there I sits in me kitchen drapping aslape sometimes wid me hed on the table.

Its hard on a poor sole, and on me Thirsdays and Soondays out the yung crachures do be bigging me to stay at home, she wid her coaxing words, and he wid his everlasting munney. Shure its ritch I'm getting wid five dollars here and the tin dollars there.

Now Minnie deer, rite me a swate letter at wunse and tell me what to do.

The family do be soospecting nuthing, for Mr. Wolley seems to have sum sacred thrubble of his own. After

Mrs. Wolley gets to bed at ate (she being a sufferer from insomnear ivery nite) I seen Mr. Wolley sneeking out of the house, like he was after going out for some meeness, and she his lorful wife innersent and unsoospecting and he an old man wid four grown luvly children.

The widder across the rode to be rooning after Mr. John and ivery nite hes aff to talk wid her about her preshus vigitibles, and wud ye belave it Minnie darlint she do be sinding over messes ivery day from her gardin "samples" she calls thim "of me own raysing."

Mr. James do be crazy wid luv for Miss Una Robbins but the poor lad do be making himsilf that oonhappy a body dare not spake to him at all at all. You see the girl do be a magnut's dorter and Mr. James is that set against all magnuts hes beside himsilf wid rage.

Ah Minnie this do be a straynge bit of coontry wid ivery body in lov wid aich uther. Over at the Dudley house there be two bold lads. Wan is very fine and ijjicated. He's Frinch—a expert shoffer as he ses. Its the hite of his ambition so he told me a few days sinse whin I be hanging out me clothes to own a small coontry shop for ortermobiles, "Boot" ses he "it taks money to buy aven a modust little place," and arsks me carelessly whether I be of the saving kind of girl. "Why musser" ses I "Its $700 Iv've poot away in the bank for me auld age." "Mon joor!" ses he, gaping at me, and it was just thin I made the acquintunce of the other lad. Hes a grate rude spalpeen, and he's after being in charge of the Dudley stables, so he tells me, ilbowing the perlite Frinchman aside.

"Good marning!" ses he "I see yure new round these parts, or you wouldnt be after spaking wid the Frinchy."

I confess Minnie I was thruly ashamed of the manner of the auld cuntry when I seen the diffrunce betwane the axshuns of museer and the other wan. I toorned a face of scorn upon the latter, picked up me baskit and marched aff in dudgin.

I'll be closing me letter now, hoping your hilth is good as this leaves me at prisint.

XVIII

Two Days Later

L arst nite whin the intyre family had retired for there hard airned slape there cum a wild ringing at the dure bell. I herd it first in me slape and yells in frite, thinking of bounding nites and burglars. I opened me dure and stuck me hed out. The hole family were assimbled in the lower hall in their nite gowns. Mr. John called up to me:

"Delia!" ses he, "wud ye plase ansser the bell."

"I will not" ses I. "Do you tak me for a gump!"

"Theres somewan at the dure" ses Miss Claire swately, "The boys arent drissed and nayther am I. Run along Delia."

"I'm dummed if I do" ses I wid indigation.

"Oh shaw" ses Mr. James, "what fools we mortals be. Whares me revolver?" ses he. "I'll go," and whistling down he desinds. We heer his voyce shouting at the closed door:

"Who's there?"

"Whats that?"

"Who?"

"A tillygram?"

"One minute," and he opened the dure.

"Who's it for?" arsks the intyre family at wanse.

"Delia!" ses he, and the family larfing wint to there rooms.

"Put it on the bottom stip darlint" ses I, "and get out of site if you plaze." I wint down and got the paper. It was as follows:

"Coming at wanse. The saints protick you darlint in the manewile. Minnie Carnavan."

This marning whin I clared aff the brikfust dishes I fownd a letter oonder Mr. Wolley's chare, which dishthressed me badly. It were as follows:

Deer sir

Do not fail to come to night early as Miss Flyte needs attention J. B.

I intinded to hand the dummed thing back to Mr. Wolley spaking at the same time me humble but contemshus opinyon of an auld sinner like himself wid a luvly lorful wife and 4 preshus children of his own. But after brikfust Mr. Wolley wint out and I sor him not agin till nite. At tin Minnie arrived. She was all exsitement.

"Now tell me widout words" ses she "what divilmint the family has been oop to."

"Divilment" ses I brideling "shure its a swate family they be. Its ashamed I am to heer you spaking langwidge aginst an innersint and luvly family like the Wolleys."

"Ah go wan" ses Minnie. "Whats the auld spalpeen been up to larst."

"If ye mane Mr. Wolley" ses I coldly, "then its a sore subjeck yeve tooched. O Minnie" ses I "the auld gintleman is a baste."

Minnie like to ate me opp wid hunger for some more words upon the subjeck.

I tuk out the letter and handed it to her widout further words. She red it throo widout spaking, but I seen her mouth and eyes popping wid exsitemint.

Joost thin Mrs. Wolley walks innersintly into me kitchin. She has sum fine lace in her hand, and she ses: "Lind me your ironing bord Delia. I'm doing these oop mesilf." Joost thin she seen Minnie, and she smiles swately—"Ah is this a frind of yours, Delia?" ses she.

Minnie got oop. I seen her studying the poor crachure for a moment, and then suddintly she walked oop to her and hild out the letter.

"I belave mam" ses she "that this will intrust you."

"What is it?" ses the madam, putting on her glarses.

"Its a letter mam" ses Minnie "to yere hoosband."

I seen her reed it throo, and aven then she had not grasped the meaning of the avil minded crachure's words, till the latter spoke oop agin:

"Are you a dummy?" asks Minnie, "Don't you see what yere auld man is after being oop to. Delia here" ses she "innersintly remarked about his sneeking out at nite to mate anuther female. The paper there reveels the auld man's inamoreeta."

I thort the auld lady wud faynt. She toorned white as milk, and I seen the paper shaking in her hand like she had the ague. But wid out condisinding a ward to eyther Minnie or mesilf she wint out the kitchen and upstares.

"Miss Carnavan" ses I, biling over wid rage, "theres a trane laving widin tin minits. Yell have plinty of time to catch it."

Minnie smiled.

"Delia darlint" ses she "did you think I'd be after thravelling sixty miles to visit you for harf an our? No darlint" ses she "I've brot me bag along and I'll be wid you for a fortnite yet."

"That you wont" ses I, "for its your bag will be out in the cinter of the strate and yersilf will follow in a sicond."

Minnie faulded her arms and fixed me wid a look of power and scorn.

"Delia Omally" ses she "the day you toorn your best frind out into the strate" ses she "will be your last. Trate me" ses she "in anny way save as a perfeck lady and I'll publish yere letter on the housetops."

It cum upon me then that like the foolish loonytick I be I'd put mesilf in Minnie's power.

"O wirrah, wirrah, wirrah!" I cryed throwing me aprun over me hed.

"Don't be after making a fool of yersilf" ses Minnie, "Have sinse, Delia mavourneen. Here I am, and here I stay."

At loonch Mr. James and John et there meel alone. Mrs. Wolley and Miss Claire were locked up in the bed room. During the meel the gintlemen spake not at all, save wanse thin Mr. John sed:

"Tak sum loonch upstares to mother and Claire, Delia" ses he, and thin after a moment: "Get that woman out of the house" ses he "as quickly as possible."

"And Delia" puts in Mr. James, conthrolling his nachelly loud voyse, "kape your mouth shut."

"Yes sor" ses I.

Mr. Wolley did not turn up again aven for dinner, and the hole family, wid the ixsipshun of the madum et in silense. Miss Claire's eyes looked red, and I seen her lips were trimbling, as tho she cud skursely kape the teers back. She cum downstares after the meel, and wispers in me eer:

"Heres a note for Mr. Dudley when he cums. I—I wont be home to-nite Delia" ses she wistfully.

"Whare are you going darlint."

"To look for father" ses she. "O Delia" ses she, "I'm afrade sumething dredful is about to happen."

"Let me go wid you darlint" ses I.

"But—the letter?" ses she, "somewan must give it to Mr. Dudley."

"I'll be plazed to do it" spoke up Minnie at wanse.

She looked at Minnie misdoutfully. Thin she wint up to her and quitely guv her the note.

"I'll trust you then!" ses she to the crachure.

About sivin in the avening the hole family, including meself set out from the house for 17 Arch Strate, which is the number on the letter paper. Mr. John and Mr. James walked on eyther side there puir mother, haulding her up by the arms, while Miss Claire and I carried hankychiffs and smilling salts. By and by we cam to the place, a little auld barn setting up against the side walk. The family guv a look at the noomber and thin walked boldly in widout nocking. There were a noysy lot of men inside. A little greesy fellow in overalls cum sontering up to Mr. John.

"What can I do for you?" ses he.

Mr. James ansers befure his brother can spake.

"Is Mr. Wolley here?" ses he bloontly.

"Shure" ses the man "he's over there wid Miss Flyte" ses he.

Mrs. Wolley stepped forward, her eyes popping out wid anger.

"Where?" ses she in such a horty tone the man stared at her wid surprise.

"There!" ses he, and poynts across the barn. "Hes having a bit of trubble wid the auld lady" ses he.

We wint across the barn, but see nothing but wan of thim red tooring cars. We've cum close to the ortermobile whin Mr. James makes a discuvery. Theres sumwan lying undernathe the masheen. He's hammering on sumthing, and theres a lited lantern on the flure beside him. Just as the discuvery was made, Mr. John likewise seen the feet; then Miss Claire recknysed her papa's boots and me his hat. Mrs. Wolley nelt down and looked under the masheen. Then she guv a scrame.

"Charles!" ses she and almost faints. Mr. Wolley cum crorling frum undernathe the ortermobile. He looks a site, wid his face cuvvered clane wid dirt and his hands dripping down wid greese.

He guv a look about him, seen us all, and drapped his mouth open wid astonishment. Joost then Mr. James burst out larfing, and the hole blessed family joyned in.

"You dummed old frord" ses Mr. James.

"What do you meen sor?" ses Mr. Wolley.

"Whares Miss Flyte?" asks Mr. John.

The auld fellow looked sheepish, and he guv a look back at the ortermobile.

"Well, ye may as well no the thruth" ses he, "Ive made a good invistmint. I've bort Miss Flyte. She's a ginooine bargin, better than anny Frinch imported car, and at quarter the price. I've been coming avenings to lern how to run and understand her. Isn't she a booty?" ses he, turning to his new infachuation.

Mrs. Wolley guv a little sob, then she run tord him jest like a child, and he guv her a kiss, and then helped her clime into the masheen.

"There's room for six" ses he. "All aboord. We'll tak Miss Flyte home."

XIX

Next Day

An ortermobile" ses Mr. Wolley at the brikfust table "is the veehicle of the moduns. Its a boom to soofering yumanity in this yumid and turribly trying and hot summers of this climut. In my opinyon" ses he, "its the greatest of modun invinshuns. Don't interrupt James" ses he, turning upon Mr. James, who was snickering noysily, "I confess" ses Mr. Wolley "that I was want sometime ago to curse the horseliss vehicle, but times are changed" ses he, "and we who wish to kape step wid the times must grow wid it. An ortermobile is a cooltivated taste its like olives. Whin first tasted we detist its flavour, but having thryed it wanse or twice we becum its ardint slaves. Jimmy" ses he "pass me anuther musk melon. John er— whats the news this marning?"

"O nothing par" ses Mr. John grinning behind his paper. "Our rickliss pressydint is waring pink pyjamas and Roosel Sage is ded."

As I was coming down the steps leading from the oopstares to the bastemint, who should I see, standing outside me kitchen door, but Mr. Moolvaney. The gintleman has his face aginst the closed dure, and hes after serrynading the lady inside—namely, me warm frind Minnie Carnavan, wid the folling sinseliss milody. I shstood still on the stares to lissen:

> *"In Dublin's fair city*
> *The girls are so pretty*
> *I wanse laid me eyes*
> *On Miss Molly Malone,*
> *Who wheeled a wheel barrow*
> *The streets broad and narrow*
> *Of cockles and mussels alive, alive, Ho!*
> *Alive, alive, Ho, ho!*
> *Alive, alive, Ho, ho!*
> *Of cockles and mussels*
> *Alive, alive, Ho!*

She was a fish monger
But shure twas no wonder
For so was her father and mother before
And they both wheeled a barrow
The streets broad and narrow
Of cockles and mussels alive, alive, Ho!

She died of the fever,
Whin no wan cud save her
And that was the ind of Miss Molly Malone
But her gost wheels her barrow
The streets broad and narrow
Of cockles and mussel alive, alive, Ho!"

As the gintleman finished I shtepped down the stares, and joost thin he toorned about and seen me caming tord him. He guv a shstart, and ses he:

"Why Delia, is it yersilf, indade? Well, well" ses he, "and shure I was after thinking it was yersilf was inside the kitchin."

I condisinded not wan ward, but I walked into me kitchin, past the false craychure, and I shoot the dure bang in his face. Minnie's seeted on a chare, shsmiling from eer to eer.

"Its a grand voyse" ses she, "I'm after lissening to. Who is the handsum gintleman Delia deer" ses she.

Joost thin the spaking chube rung out and I wint to it at wanse, and shouted oop at the tap of me voyse:

"I refoose to answser!" and wid that I shstopped up the doomed thing wid me dish towel.

XX

A Week Later

Its been a week of sorrer and disthress since Minnie Carnavan cam to visit me. Shure theres been no more peace or cumfort in me brest. She do be the most obstreprus crachure in the warld, shsticking her auld nose into ivvrywan's thrubbles and ristliss and onhappy widout shes making mischiff. Ivery nite since Minnie cum there do be thrubble of sum sort.

Shes after making the lives of the poor yung crachures disthressful, by interfeering in their innersint convysashun. Ivery nite whin I streches out me weery tired body upon me bed I lissen to the words of Minnie.

Mr. Doodley do be a rascal and a scallywag. He do be desining to rooin the life of Miss Claire. Its me thats a sinful crachure for not exposing thim to her parents and brothers, and its she Minnie Carnavan, who will seek counsil of her holy father confisser, whos no wan but hersilf. Its ny to busting she is wid keeping the sacred of the puir yung crachures love affare, and its tired I am wid me indliss attimpts to conthrol her. And now its in dred and feer I am that something dredful is about to happen.

To-nite whin Minnie was lissening at the dure, wid her eer pricked up aginst the keyhole of me private dyning-room, Mr. Dudley suddenly opens the dure. He has a bottle in his hand, and as he opens it Minnie falls at his feet.

"Is there a cat here?" ses he, and shqirts the silzer wather in her face.

XXI

Following Day

This marning whin I waked I missed Minnie Carnavan at me side. Sitting up and looking about me, I seen Minnie seeted at me table, riting a litter. She seen me whin I set up, and she faulded oop her litter and licked the invilip.

"Well Minnie Carnavan" ses I "and what are you up to at this unarthly our?"

"Hoosh, darlint!" ses she, caming to me bed, and setting down beside me. "Delia" ses she "I've dun it."

"Dun what?" ses I and I begin to have misgivings.

"I've rote" ses Minnie "to the auld gintleman."

"To Mr. Wolley" ses I a bit daft.

"No" ses she shaking her hed. "To the lad's father."

For a minit me tung faled me. I stared at the crachure in silinse. She got ap from me bed and sarched about for her hat, found it and put it on.

"Delia O'Malley" ses she "That yung Dudley fellow do be fresh as sour milk" ses she. "Its been on me conshunse iver sinse I came, mavourneen, to poonish him for his thricks. Its desaving the pretty Miss Claire hes after oop to. Trust an auld girl like Minnie Carnavan to see throo the thricks of a yung spalpeen like that."

"Minnie" ses I meekly, for theres a feer in me hart that maks me week as a kitten, "Tell me the truth darlint. Be you going to male a litter to the lad's father?"

"Indade and I am" ses Minnie bauldly, "and to mak shure" ses she "that the old dude gets it safely, I'll be me own postman and deliver it in person. Goodbye Delia mavoarneen, I'll not be coming back. Give me luv to Mr. Mulvaney."

Befure I cud git me wits thegither again, Minnie, the ritched, false crachure was gone. I herd the frunt dure close behind her.

XXII

Next Day

Oh wirrah! wirrah! wirrah! Its a sad and loansome warld and its a trecherus snake is Minnie.

Yesterday me hart was full of feers. Its menny an effort I made to relave mesilf to Miss Claire, but for pity for the puir yung creachure me tung refused to spake.

Last nite was a nite of shocks. Mr. John cum down to the bastemint and taks possisshun after dinner of me privat dining-rume. The widder do be giving him a barskit full of seeds, frish picked from her gardin, and he's after wanting he ses to sort thim out and mark the reyspictiv packages so he may know them nixt Spring whin hes going to have a fine gardin.

Miss Claire cum into me kitchin, wid her bloo eyes swimming wid teers.

"What will we do, Delia?" ses she, "John is in the dining-room to-nite, and I cant get him out."

"Now don't you be after wurriting darlint" ses I, "Shure Mr. Harry is wilcam to me kitchin."

"But John may walk in upon us" ses she despritly.

"He'd better not" ses I, and wid that I wint to the dure and called out to Mr. John:

"Will ye be good enuff to kape your disthance from me kitchin to-nite, as its private company I'm expicting."

"Very well Delia" ses he perlitely.

I wint outside to the bastemint dure, and wated in person for Mr. Harry. When he arrived, I tauld him the state of things, and he slipped into me kitchen. Miss Claire were sitting on me table, her little feet swinging in the air.

"Good avening" ses she, trying to smile and look chareful "Ye'll obsarve" ses she "the extrames to which we are driven. John holds the fort to-nite."

Mr. Harry is haulding her hands as she spakes, and watching her face like he wad ate her up.

"Had I better go thin?" ses he.

"O, if you want to" ses she, slipping down from the table, and turning away from him a bit.

"Want to!" ses he, "You don't meen that!"

"No" ses she, saftly, "I—I don't."

I thot the yung lad wud grab her, but joost thin he seen me and kept still.

Miss Claire sayses hauld of a frying pan.

"Never mind" ses she "We'll enjoy oursilves aven in the kitchen? You've never tasted me famiss fudge, have you Mr. Dudley?"

"No" ses he, looking at her pretty arms, as she rolled back the sleeves from thim.

"Well" ses she "I larned to make it in me Vassa days. Get me an aprun, Delia" ses she.

I brot her wan of her own—a little red gingum thin wid frills and pockits. She let him button it behind her, and he tuk so long she broke away larfing and blooshing.

"Now" ses she "*You* may help me. I want cream, sugar, butter and chocklett. A bit of vernilla too" ses she.

They set to work, busy and happy as childrun making mud pies. By and by the stuff was cooked, and she set him to mixing it, "and mix it stiff" ses she, "while I greese the pans."

This dun, she took a spoon and scooping out a bit she hild it to his lips. He, not looking at the fudge, but wid his eyes fixed on her, opened his mouth and took in the spoon. Then he guv a yell and down drapped the spoon.

"Oh!" ses she, turning pail, "wuz it hot? Harry!" ses she, "I *burned* you!"

"You call me Harry!" ses he, and saysed hauld of her by the arms. I was watching wid all me eyes, whin I herd the dure squake a bit. Befure I cud move tords it Miss Claire roon oop aginst it and hild it closed wid her little hands.

"The china closet, Delia!" she wispered, and I shuvved Mr. Harry into the closet and banged the dure tite. Whin we let in Mr. John he looked about him.

"Whats the matter?" ses he, "Why did you hauld me out?"

"O" ses Miss Claire, gayly, "Its a game Delia and I are playing."

He frowned and ses cauldly.

"Ye cud find bitter implyment I fancy than playing in the kitchen wid Delia. Your not a child Claire" ses he.

Shes about to spake in ansser whin the frunt dure bell run, and I saized me aprun and wint to ansser it, laving the yung peeple alone. As I reeched the upper flure, I seen Mr. Wolley turning on the lites in the hall. Then he opened the dure. A little auld gintleman wid wiskers on his cheeks and spats on his feet stud there.

"Good avening" ses he, "Mr. Wolley, I belave?"

I cud tell by Mr. Wolley's back that his face was purple. He harf closed the dure, and thin agin opened it.

"What is it you want?" ses he roodely.

"Who is it father?" ses Mr. James, comeing into the hall, then he too seen the little gintleman. The latter is spaking wid horchure and dignity.

"I cum, sor" ses he, "to—er—ask—you sir, to requist me sun to lave your house."

"I don't oonderstand you" ses Mr. Wolley cauldly.

"I resaved" ses the auld gintleman, stepping into the hall, "a nonnymuss epissle this marning. Ordinary I ignoar sich things, but me suspishuns had alreddy been aroused. I tuk it upon mesilf to play the detictive to-nite. When me sun left the house I followed him here. I saw him inter ye're place be way of the—er—bastemint" ses he hortily. "I wayted around a bit and thin desided to spake to you personally. You—er—probably appreeshiate me position" ses he. "I of coorse, shall absolutely refuse to reckynise anny foolish shcrape of the yungster— he's a mere boy" he adds loftily.

"Sir" ses Mr. Wolley, "if yure yung ass of a sun—I yuse the word advisedly" ses he "has been making a fool of himsilf over a girl in me imploy, I am not intrusted in the affare. Will you be good enuff to go to the back dure."

Wid that he's about to open the dure, when he seen me standing there.

"Delia!" ses he, "Heres your yung man's father. Just tak him into the kitchen."

Old Mr. Dudley seemed aboot to boorst, but befure he cud spake, Mr. James tuk him by the arm and lid him gintly but firmly to the kitchen dure. As I was about to follow Mr. Wolley saised hauld of me slave.

"Delia!" ses he, wispering excitedly, "is *Claire* doon stares?"

"N-no—yes—indade I don't know sir" ses I and I picked up me aprun and begun to cry into it.

We disinded to me kitchin—Mr. Wolley, Mr. James and auld Mr. Dudley, who shtumbled on the dark steps and sneezed whin he got to the bottom. In the kitchin we cum upon a straynge site. Miss Claire was standing wid her back aginst me china closet; her eyes were big and wild looking, and she kept talking to Mr. John who stud befure her.

"Go away, John! Go away!" ses she. "You shan't open the dure! You shan't! You shan't!" ses she. Then she seen us all and she guv a little cry.

"Delia! O Delia!" ses she, "don't let him. He—he soospicts sumthing," ses she, and then she poot her hed down on me shoulder and burst into teers.

I herd Mr. Harry moving in the closet, and I belave the yung chap must have herd Miss Claire weeping, for joost as she boorst into teers, he forced open the dure. For a moment he stud blinking, and thin he seen us all. He guv a look first at his father and as the auld gintleman wint tord him he drew himsilf up stiff and faced him.

"Well sir!" ses the auld fellow, choking wid rage, "so this is whare ye've been spinding your avenings—in the kitchen of these contemtyble pinny-a-liners."

"One moment" ses the lad, and suddintly he turned to Miss Claire, and poot an arm about her, but befure he cud draw her to him, Mr. James had dashed forward.

"Dam you!" ses he, "tak your hands aff me sister!" Wid that he rinched thim apart.

Yung Dudley toorned very pail, but he smiled quarely, as he moved tord the dure.

"Claire!" ses he, spaking clear over the heds of ivery wan, "raymimber darlint that we love aich other. All will cum rite yet deerest" ses he.

Thin ignoaring and pooshing past his little angry father he made his way to the bastemint dure and out.

Mr. Dudley stud a minit looking aboot him his thin lips poorsed ap in a snarling shmile. He adrissed himself to Mr. Wolley, but his eyes was on Miss Claire.

"Me sun" ses he "is yung and rash. This is not the first time I have been obleeged to cum in person to extrycate him from sich a scrape. Forchunatly" ses he "we expict him to make an airly marruge. I was talking to his finansay's father to-day and its aboot desided that the yung fokes will both be sint abrord nixt week. Good avening sir" ses he "You will not be thrubbled again" ses he. Thin, still smiling in that nasty insoolting way of his, he bowed and wint.

XXIII

NEXT DAY

After the sad ivints of the disthressful day I wint to sleep wid a hevvy hart, but sorrer a bit of paceful sleep did I get. I drimt that Minnie do be cuming to tak my place wid the Wolley family. By desateful words and ackshons she have worked upon the feelings of Miss Claire and now its me the family do be blaming for the thrubbles. I do be weeping fit to make a hart of stone ake and telling Miss Claire its me thats been a true and loving girl, a foolish victim of the sinful Minnie. But in me dream Miss Claire refoosed to look at me at all at all, and its wirrah, wirrah, I be crying in me sleep. Thin I herd somewan whispering at me eer.

"Delia! Delia!"

I set up wildly in me bed, and there I seen Miss Claire in the moonlite.

"Its I, Claire—don't be fritened, Delia" ses she.

"My God! Miss" ses I "ye do be after scaring a body. Whats the thrubble darlint" for shes neeling by me bed crying fit to brake her hart.

After a bit she looked up and ses:

"Theyve been watching me all avening. They'll niver let me be alone wid you agin. You see papa ses your to blame, and James ses that if you hadn't incoraged us to yuse your kitchen and—"

I set up and shuk me fist.

"Ef Mr. James" ses I "has anny crittersickem to be after making on a poor loan hardworking girl he'd better spake to me."

"Oh Delia" ses she "plase don't get excited. Lissen. I'm not to be house-kaper anny longer. I don't know how Harry and I will see aich other, and Oh Delia," ses she, saizing me by the shouwlder, "Did you heer him say that he—he loved me?"

"That I did darlint" ses I, "so don't you be after wurrying, for all the avil minded brothers in the warld, all the cross eyed, hard harted, black sowled, crool fathers and mothers cant coom betune a pare of swateharts whin troo love is after stipping in."

"Yes" ses she airnestly "but do you relly think he ment it?"

"*Ment* it! Its ashamed I am of you Miss Claire. Is it misdouting the woord of Mr. Dudley, you be, and he as foine a yung chap as iver stepped alive?"

The teers dryed up like magick, and she smiled as swately as a aingel. "Yes" ses she "he *did* mean it, and all *will* cum rite, for love" ses she "will shurely foind a way."

"That it will" ses I.

Well, thin she wint to bed, and I belave slipt sowndly, for her cheeks were pink as roses in the marning, and her eyes brite and luvly.

She ses "Good marning everybody" in a brave gay toan whin she cam to the brikfust table, wid the intyre family setting there and waiting in agunny for her to apeer, all suffering wid the thort of her broken hart.

Mr. John lifts oop his paper, and I seen him frowning like to brake his face behind it—hes that ankshiss to keep back a teer. Auld Mr. Wolley blew his nose like it was a throompet. Mr. James swollers his coffee red hot, and Mrs. Wolley tuk to crying to hersilf. Miss Claire guv a kiss to little Willy and wan to her father. Then she et her brikfust, beeming on everybody.

After brikfust Mrs. Wolley cam into the kitchen and guv me the orders for the day. I herd Mr. Wolley's ortermobile and looking from me winder seen him go by wid Miss Claire setting by his side, and Mr. John and James in the tonno. Mr. Billy wint out to his sand pile and Mrs. Wolley left me in peese.

It was baking day and I had jest set me bred into the pans for the fynal raysing and had opened the oven dure to see how me spunge cake was doing, whin I herd a bit of muvement at me back. I turned aboot, and let out a turrible yell, for there was me frind from the Dudley's. He do be standing in me kitchin bauld and brazen as if he belonged there, and theres a larf in his eye and on his bauld mouth too.

Now if theres wan thing bad for spoonge cake it do be a sudden bang or noyse. Its bownd to mak the finest cake fall down. Silinse is the rool wid all good cooks whin the cakes in the ooven. I throo wan look at me sponge cake and shure enuff the preshus stuff had fallen flat. Thin I rose and faced aboot on the impident yung spalpeen standing there.

"Its plane to see" ses I me hands on me hips "whare you hale frum. Its ashamed I am to acnolege you a coontryman of me own, and its lissons in foine manners ye mite be after taking" ses I "from the foine cortsheeis yung gintleman wid hoom ye have the dayly honour of assoshyating."

"Is it the frog ater ye're maning, Delia deer?" ses he.

"Me name" ses I "Is Miss O'malley, and its no time I'm after having for the loike of you." Wid that I picked up me chopping bowl and wint to wark upon the hash, a sartin loonch dispised by Mr. James whos after wanting stake wid every meel.

Mr. Mulvaney guv a larfing look at the dure lately intercated by me, then he walked over to it carelessly and shut it closed. Wid that I almost chopped me thoomb off in me rage. He cum over to the table and set upon it wid his foot a swinging. Then he leaned tord me and wispered.

"Delia darlint" ses he "what wud ye be after giving me for a love letter."

I sthopped me chopping, and guv him wan look of contimpt and scorn.

"Larry Mulvaney" ses I "if ye're wanting to no the throo value of the artucle you minshun I'll tell you. Its a clout over the eer I'd be giving you for reword" ses I and I chopped feercely.

"But suppose" ses he, leening a bit neerer "that the litter was not for *you*."

At that I stopped me chopping.

"If its Minnie ye're swate on—" but here he interrupted and took the paper from his coat and tossed it up in the air.

"Its for Miss Wolley" ses he, "and its from Mr. Harry himself."

I guv such a joomp me chopping boal wint over, wid all me prishus hash on the flure, and that the last morsil of meet in the house for loonch.

"My God, Mr. Mulvaney!" ses I, "do you mean it?"

He's very lofty now, and rising oop ses hortily:

"I'd like to see Miss Wolley if you plaze, *Miss O'Malley*" ses he wid emfasis.

"Shes out" ses I. He moved tord the dure, me aafter him, and I cort him by his slave.

"Guv it to me Larry!" I begged, "Its niver a chance the family will guv you to hand it to the puir child and shure if ye'll jest hand it to me I'll slip it into her hand widout a sole in the house gessing the trooth."

But Mr. Mulvaney put the letter into his brist pocket. Then he crossed his arms, and stares at me.

"Delia" ses he, "tell me the thruth. Are you sweet on the Frinchman?"

"Thats me personal affare, Mr. Moolvaney" ses I.

"Becorse if ye are" ses he "its only fare to let ye know hes meerly after ye-re hard airned savings. The Frinch are slick, but its a true hart ye're needing to leen upon."

"Larry Mulvaney" ses I "will you or will you not be after handing me the letter for Miss Claire?"

"On wan condition" ses he.

"Spake it" ses I.

"Guv me a kiss, darlint" ses he.

"I'll be dummed first" ses I wid indigation.

"Be dummed then" ses he, "but lissen swatehart. Mr. Dudley do be sinding Mr. Harry aff to Yurope to-morrow marning airly. Its the long distunse cure the auld gintleman do be after expicting for the lad. Now Mr. Harry has rote a litter of ixplanashuns to Miss Claire appoynting an interview. So Delia darlint its oop to you. Shall Miss Claire have the litter or shall she not?"

"My God Mr. Mulvaney" ses I "do you mean to say ye'd be holding back the litter from the puir yung thing?"

"Oonless" ses he, "you guv me a kiss."

"Tak it then" ses I "and be dummed to you."

Wid that he guv a joomp, saysed me about the waste and kissed me smack on the lips, and me riddy to sink into the airth for shame, for shure its the first time a lad do be giving me a kiss. He slipped the letter into me hand. Wid that I cam to me sinses and struck out wid me free hand. But Larry guv a larf at the smack I'm giving him and ses he:

"Delia darlint thats nothing but a love smack. Goodbye mavourneen, it'll be manny a day befure ye'll forgit the kissing I've given you."

Whin he was gone I looked about me kitchin, hardly knowing what I was seeing, wid the ixcipshun of the hash on the flure. Prisintly I herd the family coming home and I sneeked upstares hoping to get the chance of seeing Miss Claire alone. The family was on the porch, and I herd Mr. James reeding aloud from a litter in his hand:

"Deer Miss Wolley" he red, "me sun sales for Yurope per S. S. Germanya to-morrow morning at 7, and is accompanied by Miss Una Robbins and her father."

Thin followed a few more wards in which the auld scallywag congrachulated the puir yung crachure upon her iscape from a young fellow whos intinshuns were not seerius since he was all the time ingaged to another girl and he begged to remane hers fathefully S. Judd Dudley.

I left the family looking at aich other in silence and wint oop thray stips at a time to the child's room. I nocked saftly.

"Miss Claire!" I called.

I herd her sobbing inside and I called agin, "Miss Claire darlint!"

At that she called:

"Go away Delia! Go away!"

"Miss Claire!" I called wid me mouth to the keyhole "for the love of God open the dure." After a moment I herd the key turn and thin she opened it joost a crack or two. I throost in me hand and shuvved the letter in at the dure. I herd her guv a little moofled scrame and thin she was sylint. I stole away down stares and cryed in peece in me dish towel. Shure I'd be giving the bauld lad a hoondred kisses more, ef he were to ask me again for thim joost now.

XXIV

Next Day

At 4 a.m. Miss Claire cum into me room. She's all dressed and she shuk me a bit and brung me me clothes. "Dress quickly Delia" ses she, "I'm going to meet him."

"Mr. Harry?" ses I. She nods, her eyes shining both wid teers and smiles.

"Hurry!" ses she, "Its still dark and I'm afrade to go doon stares alone."

I was into me clothes in a minit and thegither we wint down the back stares. We cum to the bastemint and Miss Claire opened the back dure, and stud there waiting. There was not a bit of sun at the our, and it getting tord the fall the air do be chilly. Ivery whare we looked there seemed to be oogly gray clouds in the sky and the grass do be thick wid hevvy jew. But Miss Claire waited on at the dure, and wotched the sky, "For" ses she, "he sed at sunrise."

After a bit I seen a speck of gold cum crapping into the gray of the sky and it grew a wee bit liter. Then I seen Mr. Harry cum acrost the lon. Miss Claire seen him too and she wint out a step or two to meet him. Then he seen her and he cum running tord her, wid his arms hild wide out, and she started running tord him likewise, till they cum to aich other, and then wid never a word they were in aich other's arms, he toorning oop her face and looking at it. Thin soodently she put it doon aginst his coat (jest as I had dun wid that bold Larry) and she begun to cry saftly joost as if her hart was broken.

"Lissen Claire, me darlint" ses he, "I love you! We love aich other. The warld itself cannot divide us."

"But your going away! Your going away!" ses she, "Your going away!" and thin she looked up at him, and hild his arms tite as tho she wud not let him go.

"Only for a little wile" ses he "joost to consillerate dad. He thinks" ses he smilling scornfully, "that I'm not in airnest darlint. He offers to put me to the test. He's guv me his ward that he'll put no obsticle in me parth if I'll be gone for 6 months. Darlint" ses he "you kin wate that long for me. Otherwise I don't see what we can do. I haven't a red cent and we cuddent live on nothing."

But she still sobbed a bit aginst his coat, and she ses:

"And Una Robbins is going too. Is she—are you ingaged to her?" ses she.

"I'm ingaged to *you*" ses he so vylently that she larfed a bit, and then he tuk her hand and slipped a ring on wan of her fingies:

"Its a cheep little thing" ses he "It was me mothers. When father gave it to her they was puir—puir as—er—Delia there—he a plane worker in a masheen shop and she a cuntry teecher."

Then he kissed the finger wid the ring on, and they put there arms aboot aich other and clung a bit thegither.

"Goodbye my love!" ses he.

"Goodbye Harry!" ses she.

They seppyrated for a sicond and wint away aich from the uther. Thin they flew back to aich other and clung a bit again. And agin they seppyrated and she run tord the bastemint dure wid her hand to her throte like she was choking. She roon down the stares and I tuk her into me arms. She was shaking and trimbling like a child. Then we herd Mr. Harry's voyse;

"Claire!" he called and he cum down the stares.

"Oh God!" ses he "I cant do it" ses he. And again they clung. They broke away agin, she pushing him along.

"Goodbye" ses she. "Now go—before they cum" ses she. Then when he was gone she run up the stares and bolted the dure. I herd him at the other side, pooshing at it.

"Claire! Claire! Claire!" he called, and she inside: "Harry! Harry! Oh my love!" ses she. "Goodbye, goodbye!"

XXV

TEN DAYS LATER

G ood marning Delia" ses Mrs. Bang (the widdy acrost the strate) "Is anny wan at home?"

"Oh yes mam" ses I, litting her in throo the fly dure. "Mr. John" ses I "is after shaving his face mam" ses I "Will ye wait till hes throo?"

"Why anny of the family will do" ses she, flushing.

"Ye'll find Mr. Wolley" ses I "in the stable. Hes oondernathe the ortermobile as yushul. Mrs. Wolley is after taking her noonday syester, as Mr. James calls it and Miss Claire is in her room. Mr. James has gone to town. Mr. Billy is hilping his daddy."

"I'll see Miss Wolley" ses she hortily.

I wint oop to tell Miss Claire. She looked a bit poot out.

"Wheres John?" she arsked at wanse.

"Shaving miss" ses I.

She wint down stares, and she and the widder kissed. I wint abboot me wark doosting the dyning rume, and wiping oop the parkay flure wid a greesy cloth, manewhile linding an eer to the illygunt convysashun of the widdy. She do be fond of the sownd of her own voyce, and she threated the puir yung crachure to sooch an indless strame of sinsliss gossip as iver I had the misforthune to lissen to befure. Puir Miss Claire sat wid her chin on her hand, pretinding to lissen but heering not a word of the widdy's discurse. After a bit the widdy seemed to tak notiss of her silinse.

"You seem a bit distray this marning deer" ses she.

Miss Claire set up.

"Oh no no" ses she, "I—I'm all rite Mrs. Bangs."

The widder leened back and fanned hersilf carelissly.

"So Harry Dudley has gone" ses she, wotching Miss Claire. "It was very suddint I belave."

Miss Claire was all awake now, white and red in turn, but she sed nuthing.

"And Una Robbins is gone too" ses the widder. Suddintly she closed up her fan sharply. "Do you no" ses she "I want to say sumthing to you orful badly but I feel I haven't the rite to—not being a mimber of your family."

Joost then Mr. John cum down, looking very spry and neet wid his new shaven face and hare frish brushed.

"Hello" ses he, and shuk the widder's hands. "Are you going Claire?" ses he, for she was going tord the stares.

"If Mrs. Bangs will excuse me" ses she, "I'll finish the litter I was writing. I'll be back shortly."

Whin she was gone, Mr. John pulled up a chare and sat forward looking at the widder who opened her fan agin and was looking at the pichure on it.

"Mr. Wolley" ses she suddintly, "I'm afrade I've offinded your sister. Oh deer" ses she, "I do want to interfeer in the affares of this foolish and impracticul family. I'm shure" ses she, "If I only had the opporchunity I cud make both Claire and your brother Jimmy see the errow of their ways. Take Jimmy for instunse. He's like a prickly porkypine lately, riddy to scrach wun if wun dares to aven look at him. Look at the state of his lons. Why the grarss is a mile hy and the weeds have all cum up in the carriage drives. Why I cud tell him in a minit how to rid the drives of weeds. Salt—salt's the thing! Jest spred it on the drives. It'll kill the weeds at wunse. But ah deer me" ses she sighing hevily, "I've not the rite to advise Jimmy or cunsole Claire."

"And why have you not?" ses Mr. John camly, tho I seen him move his fingers about in the nerviss way he has.

"Why have I not the rite?" repeets the widder, opening her eyes innersintly. "Becos I'm not wan of the family" ses she.

Mr. John got up, tuk a cupple of nerviss walks acros the room, and thin soodintly wint back to the widder. He set himsilf doon on the arm of her chare leaned over her. She did'nt boodge an inch, tho I seen her get red oonder the look he guv her.

"Jane" ses he, "*be* wan of the family."

"Good grashis!" ses she, leaning back so her neck nachully fitted in the coorve of his arm, "are you *proposing* to me, Mr. Wolley?" ses she.

"Yes Jane" ses he, "I'm orfully in love wid you."

Wid that she tilted back her hed, guv him a long look, then delibritly orferred him her lips.

"Hilp yersilf John" ses she, "I'm yours."

She's larfing while she speaks, but she's crying a bit jest like ivery other woman whin he's doon wid her.

Mr. John who is a fare sized gintleman slipped down from the arm of the chare to the seet beside her. The widder is pretty ploomp hersilf and they squeezed up closely thegither, leaning aginst aich other and spooning like yung fokes, he being thirty if he's a day and she a widder.

"Now that I've got the rite to interfeer" ses she after a moment, "I'm going to do it wid a vinginse. Hold on a bit" ses she, pooshing him aff from her, "Now lissin to sense, John Wolley. Go upstares and tell Claire I want to spake to her."

"Spake to her to-morrow" ses he.

"No" ses she, shaking her hed desidedly, "John" ses she, "you an I have a whole life yet to spind thegither. I can spare you for a little wile. I came to-day upon a partikuler errant. I had sumthing to say to Claire, but first it was necissery for me to have the rite to say it. The proposul and—ah—acciptunse was a meer dyagrisshun, and wile I confiss to a shameliss weekniss for your shtyle of wooing darlint, yit I'm not to be swurved from the objick of me misshun. There! Go and get Claire, and whin I'm throo wid her cum back" ses she.

Finally, wid more airging, she injooced the puir lover to go after his sister, and whin he's brot Miss Claire back, she waves her hands airily and ses:

"Begone! I want to spake to your sister aloan."

Whin they were aloan she farely beemed upon Miss Claire, and then:

"And now to resoom deer" ses she "I was about to say sumthing to you whin your brother interripted."

"Mrs. Bangs" ses Miss Claire, wid agytashun, "*plase* don't—don't talk to me aboot—"

"Harry?" ses the widder, wid her eyes raysed up. "Why me deer" ses she, "who has a better rite to talk to you about your luvver than yure sister deer" ses she swately.

"My—" began Miss Claire, and stared at her wid round eyes. Suddintly, she saised hauld of the widder's hand and ses she wid excitement:

"You don't mean—"

The widder nodded, the teers cuming into her eyes.

"But—but he's a confirmed old bacheller" ses Miss Claire.

"Is he?" ses the widder. "Well all good things cum to an end. However John and I are beside the quiston. I merely told you as an excuse for seeming to pry into you sacred affares. Give me a kiss now and poar out your hart and sole into me sympythetic eers."

ONOTO WATANNA

Then they kissed and the widder pushed Miss Claire into a chare, and set down hersilf. Befure the girl can spake she ses hersilf crossly:

"Now will you tell me why you were such a little goose as to let Harry Dudley slip throo your fingers? My deer" ses she interrupting Miss Claire as she started in to spake. "The boy was mad—clane daft about you. Now ansser me this you notty girl, why didnt you take him?"

"I did—that is—" began Miss Claire, whin the widder grabbed her hand and looked at the ring.

"Aha!" ses she "cort you thin, did'nt I? Now" ses she "whare were your sinses under the sarcumstunses whin you let him go away at wanse—and of all things in the warld wid Una Robbins."

"*Wid* her!" ses Miss Claire.

"Yes" "It was an artful move of old S. Judd and her father. My dear, Una is the most rickluss flurt this side of heven. Why its only 3 yeers ago she was ingaged to Harry. They luvved for a moonth and broak the ingagemint a day later. Don't look so hurt. They werent achully in love—jest playing. Now Una has had her own way with men ivver sinse she wore long drisses. Thin the Wolley family moved out to the Poynt. There was a sartin rood and surly mimber of this crazy family wid a constitooshinul dislike for magnuts and there dorters. Miss Una chose to be intrusted in him, of all men. To her surprise her advanses were rebuffed. She achully disinded to pursooing him, as you no, and finully in despurashun—as I larned from her own lips—she sank so low as to insinnyvate to the loonytick that she *luved* him!"

"O" ses Miss Claire, "You meen our Jimmy."

"The terrible Jimmy!" ses the widder, nodding.

"She *told* him—"

"As good as told him."

"And he—?"

"He! Ye gods in hiven" ses the widdy throwing up her hands, "he cuvvered up his eers wid his fingys, guv a look of commingled horrow and dispare, and *ran away from her*. The follering nite" wint on the widder, "Mr. S. Judd Dudley called to see her papa, and the marning after that Miss Una was packed bag and baggage off to Yurope. Now lissen to me words of wisdom and expeerinse. If those 2 sore yung indivijools don't cum to sum sintimintul oonderstanding on this voyage out to Yurope thin my name is not Jane Bangs and will niver be Jane Wolley."

Miss Claire sed never a word, but she looked at the widder beseechingly.

"To begin wid" ses the widder, "Its all your brother John's folt. If he'd proposed to me a month ago I cud have ingineered the hole affare happily for this family. As it is now" ses she, "ye've acted like a little fool, and Harry like a big wan. Sakes alive!" ses she, "why didnt you *make* him stay at home? You had him at the sycological moment" ses she. "Do you suppose I'd have let John Wolley sale away at sooch a time? Not by a long chot. Una is sore—broosed—hartsick—hurt clane throo and throo. She's desprut. A girl in that condishun has but one resoarce—matrimunney—wid anuther fellow. Now Harry."

"Oh" ses Miss Claire, "please Mrs. Bangs don't say annything to me about him. I *know* he loves me oanly."

She cuvvered her face wid her hands convoolsively, and me shtopping in me wark in the dining-room lissening by the dure, and reddy to bat the interfeering widder on the hed wid me dooster.

"Now me deer" ses the widder, "you must counteract at wanse the evil of this long oshun voyuge. You must follow the pair at wanse to Yurope."

"I? O Mrs. Bangs, indade we arent rich people. We cudden't afford it" ses Miss Claire, "and besides, Jimmy may cross in the fall. He's been offered the London corryspundint post for the Planut."

"He'd better accipt at wanse" ses the widder promply "as for you—"

Just thin in walked Mr. John and brort an ind to the paneful interfoo. The widder found hersilf aloan wid the sintimintul gintleman looking at her tinderly. Her own face is poockered oop wod exaspenashun.

"John Wolley!" ses she, "I feel like shaking you."

"What have I dun, Jane?" ses he reproatchfully.

"Why didnt you propose to me a month ago?" ses she crossly.

XXVI

A Week Later

This marnin' wen I wint to open the door to tak in the papers a strange site greeted me eyes. "My God!" ses I aloud, "is it snowing in Orgust."

Thin I seen Mr. John. He had wun of me dish pans in his hands and it seemed to be full of holes, fer sumthing white do be scattering from the bottom of it all over the place. I throwed up me hands in horrow. Just thin I seen the widdy, and she likewise had a pan and was scattering the white doost in another place. She guv me a smile:

"Good marning Delia!" ses she, "we're goin' to surprise Mr. Jimmy. We're pooting sumthing on his drives wich will kill all grass and weeds. It's salt," ses she. "My conshunse John Wolley!" she screemed, "what are you doing?"

Mr. John was bizzy wid his pan around Miss Claire's floury hidge wich is a sorry enuff looking hidge, being that the weeds and grarss have grown out thick wid only a poor little flour to pike up its hed here and there. Mr. John do be throwing the salt wid a ginerous hand over the sad looking hidge.

"Why," ses he, "I'm killing the weeds in poor little Claire's garden."

The widdy threw doon her pan and set upon it.

"You do beat the dooch!" ses she, "why you gander," ses she, "doant you know ye'll kill the *flours* too. John Wolley, I've harf a mind to shake you and I *will* too!" ses she. Wid that she roon acrost to him, wid her hands hild out—but befure she can tooch him, he grabbed her aboot the waste, and kissed her plump on the lips.

"You retch!" ses she, "and befure Delia too! Oh-h!" ses she, and stamps her foot.

Its cleening day. Nobody but a dummed eediot wud put the desateful looking matting down on dacint flures. The doost and dirt finds a natchell place to settle down betwane the cracks. As I was rubbing it over wid a damp cloth in Mr. Wolley's stoody he came in wid the male. In wan hand he held a grate boonch of letters, in the other one ploomp fine looking litter by itsilf. He looks queer.

"Has Mr. James gone to town yet?" he asks.

"No sir" ses I. "Its riting at home he is to-day. He's in his room, sir."

"Ah!" ses the auld gintleman, and joost thin Miss Claire cum into the room.

Her cheeks are flooshed and she looks excited and ankshus.

"You have a letter for me papa, havent you?" ses she.

The auld gintleman had throost the fat letter hastily into his pocket. As Miss Claire spoke he now fussed over the boonch in his uther hand.

"Let me see" ses he, going over thim, "No—theres nuthing my deer" ses he.

She seemed so disappoynted that for a moment she joost stared at the auld gintleman. Then she ses gintly:

"Papa, wasnt there an English male in yisterday?"

"I belave there was" ses he.

She put out her hand impetchussly and ses she:

"Let *me* see, papa?"

She wint over the letters wan be wan. She picked out wan little roll, and she ses:

"Nothing—nothing at all for me—ixcipt this." Thin she wint out from the room suddintly.

The auld gintleman looked after her wid a look fool of compashun and guilt. Then he sneeked out of the room.

"You auld divil!" ses I to mesilf, "Its a letter ye've got in your pockit for Miss Claire, and the puir thing shull have it if I have to turn thafe to get it for her."

Wid that I wint after the auld rascal. I hurd the dure of Mr. James's room shut, and I wint into the bathroom adjyning, and wid wan eer to the dure I lissened.

"James—" ses Mr. Wolley stipping in.

"What the—" began Mr. James and I herd him hopping up in his seet. "I'm bizzy father" ses he. "I must get out this artuckle at latest by noon to-day" ses he "What is it? What is it?"

"James" ses Mr. Wolley, "I'm afrade yure sister—"

"For hivin's sake father" ses the lad "hoory up. Jest what is it?"

There was silinse for a moment, juring which I knowed from instink Mr. Wolley had tuk out Miss Claire's litter and shown it to his son. I prissed up close aginst the dure, but the key was inside and I cud see not a thing. Then I herd Mr. Wolley say:

"You see it is as we feered. They are corry—"

"Hauld on!" ses Mr. James lowering his voyce, and again there followed a sylinse. Suddintly the dure flew open and I fell upon me face into the room. Mr. James saized me by the neck of me gown and hauled me oop.

"Delia!" ses he, "ef I ever catch you at sich a thrick again, I'll—I'll throw you out of the winder" ses he. "Now git!" ses he, and I sloonk aff in shame.

I was coming down the stares, skurce looking whare I wint, whin all of a suddint I seen sumthing which sint me hart flying into me mouth. There by the winder was Miss Claire stritched out on the floor. Her face looked orful white, and for a moment the dredful thort cam into me hed that the poor yung thing was ded. I screamed wid frite and agunny, and I joomped doon the rist of the stares and run to the child. The paper was on the floor beside her—a torn peece of noospaper and I seen the pincil marks in blue upon it. The family cam rooshing down whin they herd me scream and at the site of Miss Claire they all seemed about to faynt also. Mrs. Wolley guv a friteful scream, and Mr. John throo his arms aboot her and put her into a chare. Mr. James picked up the bit of paper, turned it over and red:

> "Mr. and Mrs. Barclay Robbins announces the ingagement of their dorter, Miss Una, to Mr. Harry Judd Dudley, son of S. Judd Dudley of New York. The widding will tak place Choosday the 21st of October."

There was silince then, the hole family looking at aich other and then at puir Miss Claire. Then Mr. Wolley spoke, and his auld voyce trimbled.

"Boys" ses he, "carry your sister gintly to her room."

It were a sorry loonch the family et. Mr. John skurcely opened his mouth wanse to spake, and Mr. James spoke only wanse. He sed camly:

"Father" ses he "I've desided to refuse the London corryspondunt job."

Mr. Wolley turned feercely upon little innersint Billy:

"Billy" ses he, "ef you play wid yure salt at the table wanse again" ses he, "I'll tak me razer strap to you."

Thin he tuk 2 angry bits at me rolls, and stomped oot to the frunt porch. Looking out I seen him scowling at the Dudley house.

Neyther Miss Claire or her mother cum doon to loonch.

"Mr. John" ses I whin all had left the table ixcipt him: "Is Miss Claire all rite now?"

He put his fingers into the fingy bowl and wiped them thortfully.

"I'm going across the street" ses he, "I belave Jane can make it all rite" ses he, as if spaking to himsilf.

I was washing the family dishes in the butler's pantry, when I seen Miss Claire cum saftly doon the stares. She'd got on a little pink drissing gown over her nite dress and her long yillow hare was hanging all aboot her. She seen me looking at her, but whin I wint forward to spake to her she made a little impashunt moshun wid her hand and I stud back. She wint over to the tillyfone and guv a number:

Then I herd her say:

"Is this the Planet? Yiss, Well I want the idiotoryell departmint. Hello" ses she, "I want to spake to Mr. Allun—Allun—I sed Allun" ses she gitting exsited, and she spelled the name. She wated a bit, and thin: "Good-morning Mr. Allen" ses she, "This is Miss Wolley— Wolley—Claire Wolley," ses she. "Now lissen—announce me ingagemint in to-morrow marning's *Planut*—and say that I deny it but its so" ses she beginning to larf hysturically. "Whats that?" ses she, "Oh his name—his name you said. Why how silly of me. His name is—er—Stevin Vandybilt. Oh thank you" ses she. "*I* hope so too" ses she. "Whats that? Oh thanks. Yes, yes of coarse hes wan of *the* Vandybilts. Goodbye."

She toorned aboot, an I seen her grarsp hold of the back of a chare. She leaned aginst it, and she begun to shake, and thin she larfed. She larfed so hard and queerly that she fell upon her knees. Then I ran oop to her, and thried to put me arms about her, but she guv me a feerce poosh, and ses she wid her eyes flushing:

"Don't tooch me! Don't dare put yure hand upon me. Its all yure folt. It was you who brort us thegither. It was you who—Ah hahahahaha!" ses she, lafing and crying thegither.

The widder cam in wid Mr. John and she run over to Miss Claire wid her arms spred out.

"O me deer! me deer!" ses she, "I worned you—I told you."

But Miss Claire has cum back to her sinses.

"Mrs. Bangs" ses she "I am not in need of inny sympithy. Excuse me. Good marning" ses she, and wint up the stares and back to her room. We hurd the dure banged tite.

The widder burst into teers, and as fur me, puir loan onhappy crachure that I be I betuk mesilf to me ritched kitchen and cryed me hart out into me clane starched table aprun.

I thort the day wud niver ind and whin the Frinch charfer from the Dudleys came over, its small eers I had for his foine spache.

"Museer" ses I "its a hart broken wumman I am, and its small cumfut I'm taking in yer perlite langwidge to-nite."

"Mumsell Delia" ses he, "belave me on me sacred onor, I adoar you wid me hart and soal. Be mine" ses he.

Mr. Mulvaney caming in joost thin, guv a larf at the Frinchman, which made the puir museer furyiss.

"Mumsell" ses he, "I be not of the for chune hoonting sort as yere frind there" ses he.

"Whats that ye're after saying" ses Larry, at wanse. "Did you spake me name?" ses he.

The Frinchman stud his grownd bravely, and droring himsilf prowdly up faced Mr. Moolvaney wid a stare.

"Jaccuse" ses he, "Museer Mulvaney of wooing the lady wid his eye on her forchune. Jaccuse"—ses he, but Mr. Mulvaney had him by the collar of his coat and museer was setting outside on the lon befure I cud rise to protist. Whin Mr. Mulvaney cam back I'm that insinsed wid his avil manners and the revylashun of his meen and greedy caracter that I skurcely cud aven look at him.

"Mr. Mulvaney" ses I "its a puir hard working girl I am, and its a mistake ye're making in yure for chune hoonting hart whin ye think I'm after being rich. Ah go!" ses I, "I'm doon wid avery wan of you."

And I wint opp to me milincully room, me hart sore and aking, for Miss Claire do be hating me feercely now, and Larry Mulvaney is no better than the Frinchman, but is after me puir bit of forchune. Ah wirrah, wirrah, wirrah! Its a sorry day whin me muther bore me.

XXVII

THE NEXT DAY

Miss Claire was down at brikfust brite and airly. I seen her setting at her plate—waiting for the family to appeer. Her eyes and cheeks wuz unnatshully brite.

Mr. John cam in first. He wint over to her chare and guv her a rell luving kiss.

"Go to your seet John" ses she "I've sumthing to show you." Wid that she pushes over the paper to him and intercates a place wid her finger.

"Claire!" ses he starting oop "My dear girl," ses he, "whot on airth doos this mane."

Jist thin Mr. James cum in and Mr. Wolley close on his heels— Miss Claire picked up the paper and parsses it along gayly to Mr. James saying as she duss so:

"It's *only* the enouncemint of me ingagement" ses she.

"The whot!" ses Mr. Wolley.

Mr. James' face looked tired and haggard and his big eyes have lost there fighting look. He turned them orlmost sadly on his sister.

"Claire," ses he, "you're—you're acting hastily," ses he.

"Not at all," ses she, smiling—over her cup of corfee. "I've nown Mr. Vandybilt iver since I wuz at Vassa. I niver told any of you aboot it—but—but—we've practically bin ingaged—fer yeers—thet is not formally."

The family sed nothing and I wint to ansser the door as the bell wuz ringing furyissly. The widder cum in and wint widout being invited strate to the dining-room. She also has a paper in her hand and widout a word to the rest of the famly she pulled oop a chare and sat doon beside Miss Claire.

"Claire" ses she "I had just finished reeding a letter from Una Robbins when I chanced to glance at me paper. I saw the announcemint. Child, whot does it *meen*?"

"Why," ses Miss Claire smiling brillyuntly—"Exackly whot it ses."

The widder luked soospishus and thin she ses wid emfasis:

"Well I'll not congratulate you. It's a mistake—all rong," ses she, "Oh deer! oh deer! Oh deer!"

She turned suddintly upon Mr. James.

"Jimmy," ses she, "I notissed just now when I minshuned the name of Una Robbins that you winced a bit. Now look here boy" ses she "Una *may be* ingaged to Harry—and she may marry him too—but let me tell you" ses she, "a girl who's ingaged to wan man and rites ten pages about anuther man to a frind is worth invistygating. Take my advice, Jimmy deer," ses she "and go to Londoon town post haste. What are *you* doing Claire?" ses she, for the girl has gone to the desk in the hall and is marking the paper wid a red pencil. She rolled it oop and rote upon the cover, thin she wint over to her father—

"Papa!" ses she, "There's *my* mail. Hurry it aff, won't you," ses she.

XXVIII

Next Day

I was doing up the bed in Mr. Wolley's room whin Miss Claire walked in. She wint into her father's closet and cam out wid her arms fool of his cotes. These she set on the bed and camly wint to wark sarching throo his pockits. After a bit she cam upon what shes looking for—the fat litter which arrived yesterday. She held it in her hand a sicond her eyes closing oop. Thin suddintly she wint over to the fire place. She toar the litter acrosst, invillip and all, then neeling throo it into the grate and set it on fire. Joost thin her father cam in, and she looked oop at him and smiles.

"Why Claire" ses he, "what are you doing?"

"Papa" ses she, "sumthing told me that *he* had ritten. I soospected you yisterday. I've just been burning the litter. Hereafter papa" ses she, "whin anny more such litters cum, trate thim in the same way—*burn thim—burn them—burn them*" ses she.

Thin she stared up at him wid her cheeks all red and feverish, and she cryed out suddintly, "Oh papa! papa!" ses she, crowched doon on the harth and sobbed wid her face all ooncuvvered and the teers joost poring down.

"My puir Claire!" ses the auld man brokenly; then he seen me and spoke in a feerce voyce:

"Lave the room Delia!" ses he.

This arfternoon Mrs. Wolley cum down to the kitchen. She's very figitty and nerviss and she skurce looked me in the face at all.

"Delia" ses she, "yure moonth is oop on the 12th. We've decided to let you go."

I cudn't spake at all fur the loomp in me mouth. I wint to the sink and foosed aboot wid the dishes.

Mrs. Wolley continued unasily.

"You understand Delia" ses she, "we've no complaint to make aboot you. You're a good cook and excellent in ivery way—but Claire—Claire isn't very well and we must humour the child. The fack is Delia, the very site of you seems to recall a sartin unplissant person to her mimmry."

"Oh ma'am," ses I, "indade I wud cut me hed orf for Miss Claire, but indade," ses I, "it's sad I'd be to lave the child as such a time. Let me stay ma'am, if oanly till ye go to town in October."

"No" ses she, shaking her hed, "it's better not."

I set down and thort the matter over. Why shud I be turned out in this fashun ses I to mesilf. It's a shame, a crool shame it is. It was thin Mr. Mulvaney cum sontring in and befure I know wat I'm about I'm telling him the story of me sorrers.

"Bad cess to thim all!" ses he, "they desarve to lose a fine girl like you, Delia, and if ye'd lissen to my airging it's laving thim ye'd be to-day and stipping wid me over to Father Dugan's. These Wolleys do be a trubblesum famly. Shure they've toorned the hole poynt oopside doon wid thrubble. I heer that the Robbins are arfter being beside thimsilves wid feer of Mr. James. Now Delia" ses he, "ef ye'll not be heering to the praste, thin it's anuther bit of advice I'm arfter giving you. Stip across to the Widdy Bangs' house," ses he, "and tell her your thrubbles," ses he. "I'll bet me job aginst the Frinchman's that she'll fix you all rite wid the family."

So I wint over to the widdys house. A spoonky little culloured maid opened the frunt dure. She guv a luk at me face—ignoring me best clothes on me body and ses she:

"Go to the back dure," ses she. "*I* recave me collars there."

"It's Mrs. Bangs" ses I "I want to see."

"Mrs. Bangs," ses she, "is ingaged wid Mr. Wolley."

I heerd the widdy's voyce inside and prisintly she cum oot and ses:

"Hoo is it Lilly," ses she, (My God! The Nigger's name was Lilly and she black as hell).

"Why, it's Delia!" sez the widdy.

"Can I spake to you a minnit, mam!" ses I.

"Why certinly Delia. Whot is it," ses she.

I wint to throw me aprun over me hed but fownd I'd left it at home, so I set up a paneful cry widout it. "Oh wirrah! wirrah!" ses I, "it wuz an avil day whin I crossed the oshun. Oh mam" sez I, "it's a cruel warld and peeple do be hard on a poor hardwarking crachure wid niver a frind in the world."

The widdy looked as if she were aboot to larf, but she's that sorry fer me she controlled hersilf. She poot her hand on me shoulder and ses she kindly:

"Cum! What is it, Delia? my deer?"

"Mrs. Wolley do be arfter firing me, Mrs. Bangs," ses I, "and all because I'm odyiss in the site of Miss Claire and all because I hilped her meet Mr. Harry Doodly—the crool faithless good-for-nothing villyun" ses I.

"You poor crachure," ses she, "and you want me to spake fur you. Why, of coorse I will. I'll go rite over and appeel to Claire's sinse of justiss."

Whin I was gitting ondrissed to-nite I herd me dure opening, and I guv a lowd yill, fer I'm in me chimmy aloan. As Miss Clair cum in, I rooshed into me closet, and I spoak to the child frum behind the harf closed dure.

"What is it darlint?" ses I "Its ashamed I am fur you to see me in dishabeel and me wid twinty bunyuns on me feet and moles on me ligs and arms. What is it swatehart?"

"Delia" ses she in the gintlest voyce, "Plase forgive me for my croolty and ingratichude. I've been thortless and oongrateful too" ses she, spaking into the closet, "for aven oonder the sircumstunses I don't regret—Harry. So you'll stay—won't you Delia?" ses she.

"Stay miss?" ses I, "Why darlint you cuddent roon me out wid a steem roller."

XXIX

ANOTHER DAY

It do be thray weeks to-day sinse Miss Claire's after announsing her ingagemint to Mr. Vandybilt. The family kept silinse upon the subjeck. Its a straynge and sad house its after being now.

Both Mr. John and James wint back to there rayspictif places in the city on Siptimber 1st after having spint the intyre summer doing there fine riting at the hoose.

Mr. James do be a famiss riter and theres hardly a paper pooblished but has a pichure of himself looking out frum the frunt page, bauld and agrissive looking, for shure the lad do have his back oop aginst the intyre warld. Hes joyned the Soshilist and Anykist ordher I'm after reeding in the papers, and its intinded by him (ses wan of the papers, which always nos a person's plans befure there made) to live in the slooms for the rist of his life, devoating himsilf to sittlemint wark amang the Rooshin Jews.

Mr. Wolley's masheen broak down aboot a fortnite ago, and the auld gintleman is like a child widout his favrite toy. He do be wayting ivery day for the new carbureater to arrive, and manewile he spinds all his time fooling aboot wid the masheen that isn't rooning anny longer. Mrs. Wolley has dridful narviss hidakes, injooced so she told me in confydunse as mooch by her wurry over Miss Claire as frum anny uther cause.

As for Miss Claire hersilf. Puir child! She do be that quite and shrinking in her ways. Theres skurcely a site I'm getting of the child ixcipt at meal times.

Its not warth intering up the milincully ivints of the sad days, and shure I'll be glad indade whin we move back to town in a few weeks now.

There be no troo Nites abownding in this sad and loansum country, for the Nites are an avarashus lot. Since the news wint abrord that I'm having me little bit of forchune in the bank, I've been pestered wid the dummed forchune hoonters till I begin to look wid soospischun on ivery dummed man that spakes to me at all.

Ah, its a sad thing to be ritch in these days, for the lads cum acoorting wid wan eye on yere pockit and the ither on yere face. Since museer infarmed me of the greedy hart of Mr. Mulvaney its never a sivil ward I've handed the lad since, and he pretinding to be beside himsilf wid disthress and begging me ivery day to go wid him to the praste.

"Mr. Mulvaney" ses I, "whin Delia O'Malley is reddy to marry she'll be choosing a thrifty lad wid a forchune larger than her own. Do you tak me for a nigger?" arsks I. "Ivery dummed one of those unforchunt crachures do be washing after marruge, handing over there hardairned wages to the cauld-harted goomps theyve been loonyticks enuff to marry. Larry Mulvaney" ses I, "Its a smart lad ye are, but Delia O'Malley sees throo yere thricks."

"Delia, me darlint" ses he, wid such airnestness I'm almost like to belave him, "I wish" ses he, "ye'd tak yere munney frum the bank and drap it into the well" ses he. "Its you I want" ses he, "not yer auld munney."

"Mr. Mulvaney" ses I cauldly, "Anny wan but an eediot" ses I "cud fish up a bit of munney put doon in a well."

To musseer I likewise ixprissed mesilf consarning forchune hoonters in gineral and furringer in pertickler.

"Museer" ses I "I oonderstand its the custum in yure cuntry for the wimmen to guv over there bit of a forchune to there worthliss hoosbunds?"

"May but me share Mumsell Delia" ses he, "Is it not thin a grand custom? Think sharee" ses he, "Hoo shud be the custoadyun of the joynt wilth of such a onion if not the hed of the family. Why sharee" ses he, sharee being Frinch for mavorneen, "It is as it shud be."

"Museer" ses I, "I may be auld-fashuned, but I shtand here riddy to state the following facks. I'm a hard warking girl and befure I'd see me hard airned savings parss into the hands of a good-fur-nothing disiloot Frinch husbund I'd throw it into purgatry and burn it oop insted. Good marning museer" ses I "Will you plase ixcuse me this avening."

XXX

A Week Later

I got ap this marning at siven. While wiping me face after giving it a good sousing wid warter, I chanst to look from me winder. I seen the rane poaring down frum a gray and milincully sky.

"Its a sad day its going to be to-day" ses I to mesilf, little noing the throoth of the matter. The day itsilf to be shure passed away as yushil. I warked and cooked. The family et. The house looked dark and gloomy, and I belave it cheered us all up a bit whin I'm toorning on the lites.

After dinner I planned to rite to Minny, and so was hurrying throo the washing of me pots and pans in the sink whin I herd me bastemint dure open and close wid a bang, and ses I to mesilf: "Its that bauld Larry Mulvaney walking into me kitchin widout the dacinsy aven of nocking." So I kipt me contemshus back toorned aven whin the stips cam along throo the bastemint hall and paused at me kitchin dure. Thin I herd a voyce spaking me name.

"Delia!"

I toorned aboot, and thin I lit out a turrible yell which I shoot up quickly be throosting me dishcloth into me open mouth. For there sthtanding in me kitchin, his long coat dripping wid water, the collar toorned up about his eers, and his soft filt hat pooled doon over his eyes was Mr. Harry Dudley himsilf. His eyes looked straynge, and his face was all oonshavin aboot the chin. He cum tords me quickly and clapped his hand on me showlder. If I hadent recknissed the lad, shure I'd be taking him for a thramp.

"Go upstares" ses he, "and bring Claire—Miss Wolley doon. I want" ses he, "to see her at wanse."

"Yes sir" ses I trimbling wid excitemint, for he do have the wild look of a mainyack in his eye.

I rooshed up the stares to Miss Claire's room, and forgitting to nock wint in.

"Miss Claire" ses I, me breth cuming in gasps, "w-wud ye be so kind to step into me kitchin a moment."

She stud up, looking at me surprysed and bewildyed.

"Whats the matter Delia?" ses she.

"Plase hilp me, Miss Claire" ses I "For God's sake" ses I gitting excited, "cum down at wanse."

"Are you and Larry fighting again" ses she. "What can I do this time?" ses she, but she let me lead her along doon the stares, and thegither we cum to the bastemint. Me kitchin dure was open and I belave she seen Mr. Harry setting there befure shes cum into the room, fur all of a suddint she guv a turrible start and pulled away frum me arm, trying to go back oop the stares. At that I called:

"Mr. Harry!" and then he stud up, and she wint slowly tord him. They stud for a moment looking at aich uther widout spaking a wurd. Then he tuk his hat aff and put it on the table, and she thried to spake and cuddent say a ward. I seen her looking wid horror at his dripping clothes and wite haggud face, and I belave she guv a little sob for so it sownded. Thin he spake in a saft voyce, looking at her full in the eyes.

"Claire" ses he "I took a boat back fur home harf an hour after yure letter and that—that—cursed paper came" ses he. Thin he stapped a bit. "I've cum up strate from the steemer now. I havent been home. Tell me the trooth" ses he. "Why did you treat me in that way?" ses he.

She did not ansser, but the colur cum back to her pale face and she raysed up her hed prowdly.

"Am I to belave" ses he "that *you* wud throw me over for a chap wid more munney. Claire!" He wint a step tord her, his hands hild out. "For God's sake" ses he "tell me that it is all sum horribul mistake."

She wint back frum him.

"Mr. Dudley" ses she. "I quistshun yure rite to inquire into me affares, but if you wish me simply to verryfy the announcemint of me ingagemint to Mr. Vandybilt, I do so."

He guv a grone, and set down in the chare, leening forward wid his hands prissed thegither. Miss Claire stud there cauldly, but she did not look at Mr. Harry anny more.

Suddintly he throo back his hed and guv a little larf. Thin he got up and picked up his hat and moved tord the dure.

"Stop!" ses Miss Claire, toorning rownd suddintly, "wait wan minit" ses she. "Ansser me this Mr. Dudley," ses she. "What rite have you, an ingaged man, to spake to me in such a way?"

"What rite have *I*" ses he, looking biterly amoosed "Yes" ses he, "throo, I *was* ingaged wance, Miss Wolley. I belave" ses he, "I guv you me muther's ring."

"No!" ses she, and her voyce rung out pashunutly "Not that! I don't meen that ingagemint—ef you considered it ever such" ses she, and her voyce catched oop in her throte which she hild wid her hand, "I mean" ses she, "yure ingagemint to Una Robbins. You—"

He looked so flabbygasted that she stopped.

"What do you mean?" ses he.

"Oh you know, you know" ses she. "Befure you were gone a fortnite" ses she "yure ingagemint was annownced." "My ingage—Claire!" ses he horsely, and he saized hold of her hand vilintly. "Theres sum misurable mistake. You've been misled, desaved."

"No, no, no" ses she struggling to free her hands, which he let go suddintly. "It was annownsed" ses she. "You know it. You know it."

"Announced whare?" ses he cauldly.

"In the London Queen."

"When!"

"I don't—"

It was thin I spoke up, for I'd taken the paper frum the recipshun hall the day Miss Claire faynted, intinding to burn the dummed thing. I now guv it to Mr. Harry. He toorned it over contemshusly. Thin he guv the paper a long scrootiny. Finally he looked up and fixed his eyes on Miss Claire. His voyce is very cam and quiet.

"This notiss" ses he, "was published exactly three and a half yeers ago. If you had aven taken the thrubble to examine the paper you wud have seen that, aven tho the date is torn aff. Thank you for your faith in me" ses he. "Who sent this I do not no. Probably my father. And now" ses he "theres nothing more to say. I hope you will be happy Claire. I don't know Vandybilt" ses he, "but—still I hope you will be happy. Good-nite" ses he, and he wint oot of the dure, widout looking at her again. I seen her wake oop like wan coming out of a transe. She guv a little moan, and thin she wint following after him to the hall.

"Harry! Harry!" she called in the dark. I herd him stop short, and thin her voyce agin. "Oh forgive me" ses she. "I—I—faynted at the time. I never saw the paper again. My—my hart was broken, for I loved you so—I love you yet" ses she.

And thin I herd him joomp tord her.

"But yure ingagemint to Vandybilt" ses he horsely.

"Theres *no* Mr. Vandybilt" ses she, "I—I made it up" ses she, and then she stopped spaking and crying too for he's got his arms aboot her and her lips closed oop wid his.

I toorned away and sobbed. How long they stud I do not know, but it was a long time whin finnily he starts to spake again:

"Claire—my darlint!" ses he, and thin again they are silint.

Then after awile.

"What will we do?" ses she, "we—we cant give aich uther up now."

He larfed like a boy.

"Give aich uther up" ses he, "Why we belong to aich uther. Now lissen darlint. I havent a cent to me name. Dad has kept me practicully pinnyliss lately, but I maniged to borrer enuff to git back here. I've niver dun a stroke of work in me life, but I've a good ijjicashun—I'm yung, strong and willing. I've been offered a job out West wid a stepbruther of me muther's, and we'll go there as soon as I can rayse the munney to take us. Oh my little love" ses he, "I only wish I cud take you away to-nite and kape you wid me always."

"Take me—take me Harry" ses she, clinging about his neck, "Let us go to-nite."

"I wish we cud" ses he, "but look," and he drew her into the lite of me kitchin and toorned out all his pockits and showed her how imty they was. It was then a brillyunt thort cum into the hed of Delia O'Malley.

"Mr. Harry" ses I interrupting, "will you be excoosing me for putting a quischun?"

"What is it Delia" ses he kindly.

"How mooch is it ye're nading?" ses I.

He smiled.

"A few hundred only" ses he. "Jest enuff for our imejit ixpinses. Its absurd but I havent a red cent" ses he. "I'll borrer or steel it if I have to" ses he, trying to larf, the puir lad.

"Mr. Dudley" ses I, "Will ye be doing a puir loan hardwarking girl a favour?"

"Why certinly" ses he. "What can I do for you?"

"Its siven hundred dollars I'm after having in me stocking. I droo it oot of the bank oanly a day or two ago, fur the dummed welth do be the bane of me existunse. Shure I'll nivver know anny pace of mind so long as I'm ritch. Mr. Mulvaney do protist that he wishes me munney soonk in hell, and museer is after saying he loves me better than me bagatell. Its tisting the lads I'd be doing, and ef ye'll do me the favour of accipting me bit of munney—"

"Oh Delia!" ses Miss Claire.

"No, no" ses Mr. Harry at wanse, but she pulled down his face, and wispered in his eer, and suddintly he toorned and beemed at me.

"Very good! Delia" ses he, "guv me the munney."

I wint into the china closet and tuk it frum me stocking—thin I brort it over to Mr. Harry. He hild on to me hand arfter taking it, and his voyce trimbled a bit.

"Yere a foine woman" ses he, "and its a lucky chap who gets you. Your bit of munney" ses he, "will be ten times its size whin it reeches you again."

"Now Claire darlint" ses he, and he looks at her wid shining eyes, hers smiling back at him, "Will you go wid me—*to-nite*?"

"Give me five minits" ses she, smiling saftly, "to get me hat and coat."

"Make it 2" ses he, and let her go.

He put his watch on the table. Arfter a sicond:

"One minit!" ses he, and woches the stares. "One and a harf" ses he, and joost thin the bastemint dure bell rung, and I let in both museer and Larry Mulvaney, pushing and ilboing by aich uther.

"Two minits" ses Mr. Harry, and then we herd the dure on top of the bastemint steps open, and Miss Claire cum steeling down, her coat and hat in her hand.

"They are all in there rooms" ses she wispering. Then she seen Museer and Larry, both of them wid there mouths and eyes gaping at Mr. Harry. He was smiling quarely and he toorned to museer:

"Alfonse!" ses he, "ye've arrived in the nich of time. I want you" ses he "to go back to our place and get riddy the big Pinkard. We'll be over in a sicond."

Museer bowed, but he histated a minit.

"Well?" ses Mr. Harry, "What are you waiting for?"

"Whare is it Museer wishes to go" ses the Frinchman rubbing his hands narvissly thegither, and giving a look at Miss Claire.

"To New Rosette" ses Mr. Harry smiling, "I know a parson there" ses he, "will do it in a jiffy. His name's Hammond" ses he, and then suddintly he turned tord me. "And by the way Alfonse" ses he, "Puir Delia here will be ixpicting you back airly. Shes lost her little forchune."

"Mon Joor! Sacrey! Dam!" ses Museer and looked at me wid his eyes boolging, then he stamped oot, swaring tarribly in Frinch.

Larry guv me wan look, then he begun to wissel, excusing himsilf a moment after to Miss Claire.

Mr. Harry hilped Miss Claire on wid her coat, and buttoned it up snug to her chin. "For" ses he "its cold and raining, and we have quite a trip to make" ses he.

Thin we all started out frum the house Mr. Dudley almost carrying Miss Claire over the wet lon and Larry Mulvaney grasping me titely by the arm.

We got into the Dudley driveway and cum up befure the grate barn. Then we seen museer at the tillyfone. Hes spaking franticully harf in Frinch and harf in English. Mr. Harry putrifyes him wid a look and he drapt the tillyfone and turned sowerly to the big ortermobile, pretinding to start it. Mr. Harry helped Miss Claire into the tonno, thin the Frinchman climed in frunt. Mr. Harry foosed a bit wid the masheenery, then he joomped in beside the Frinchman, and all of a suddint he seesed the weel frum the Frinchman's hands, guv a toot to his horn, and wint flying out of the barn dure, joost as auld Mr. Dudley cum rooning frum the house waving his hands and showting: "Alfonse! Alfonse!"

He cum into the barn farely choking wid rage. The nixt moment he seen Larry and me.

"Larry" ses he, and he climed into the uther masheen, standing there. "Overtake those loonyticks" ses he, "and I'll make you a ritch man."

"I will" ses Larry "I kin beet anny Frinchman living."

I fownd me way home aloan, Larry the crool harted miscreent wid his avoreeshus hart having obeyed the order of Mr. Dudley. As I cum into me kitchin I fownd the hole Wolley family, wid the ixcipshun of Mrs. Wolley and the babby, waiting for me.

"Whare have you been?" shouted Mr. James, and Mr. Wolley guv me a look fit to kill me.

"Theres no yuse attimting to desave us Delia" ses Mr. John quietly, the only cam wan of the boonch, "The Dudley charfer tillyfoned us the facks a minit sense. Now, whares Claire. I presoom" ses he, "they were stopped in time?"

"Not by a dummed site sir" ses I, gitting turribly inraged wid the site of the thray strapping men pursooing the puir yung luving harted crachures. "They've got a good start of that desateful Larry Mulvaney, and Mr. Harry himsilf has got the wheel."

Mr. Wolley let out a larf of scorn.

"Boys" ses he, "me new carbureater arrived yistiday. We'll ovetake that Frinch car in harf an our."

Wid that they all wint for the barn, got out the car and in there exsitemint let me climb in wid them also.

Well, we wint spinning at a turrible speed along the auld Boston Post Road but never a site did we get of the Dudley Frinch car.

The roads was turrible for the stiddy rains of the larst week do be cutting it up into ditches, and manny a time me hart was in me mouth feering we'd be going into the gutter. The nite was pitch dark and the ilictrick lites over harf the road being out wid the lightning.

As we cam whissing along over a wild and loansum cuntry we herd a straynge sownd, like samewan hollering for hilp, and then we seen a lite ahed. We roon up beside it and there in the road was anuther masheen. It was so dark we cud not see the gintleman but whin I herd his voyce I guv a start.

"Can you tak me as far as New Rosette" ses he. "I'm soaking wet and cold" ses he, "and me dammed man don't understand the meckaneesm of this masheen."

"Climb in" ses Mr. Wolley gruffly, and he got in at the back.

We started aff again, and by and by we cam at last to New Rosette. We wint feeling our way arownd the strates, wid the rain beeting doon upon our lether top and the thoonder and lightning litting out a crack avery wanse in a wile.

Thin suddintly we cam to a stop. Theres a gas lite burning in the strate, and setting back a bit from the road on a lumpy bit of lon I seen what looked like a church and at its very dure indade there stud the grate Frinch ortermobile of Mr. Dudley. But neyther Miss Claire or Mr. Harry was inside it. The gintleman guv a gront, and thin ses he:

"Excuse me sir, allow me to get out here."

Mr. Wolley has turned aboot, and now he leened over the back of the seet and stuck his face close up to his gest's. Then at wanse they recknised aich other. The boys too soospicted the truth at wanse. Mr. Dudley himself was for joomping clane out of the masheen, but Mr. John opened the dure wid dignuty, and perlitely hilped him to alite.

We wint all walking up the path to the choorch, and we cud see theres a bit of lite burning inside. We wint into the holy place, which is all very still and quiet wid only a bit of dim lite up near the altar, but under the lite we sor the luvvers, neeling side be side.

Neyther Mr. Dudley or Mr. Wolley spoke a wurd. They joost stud back and let the praste finish the wurds. Thin I seen two gintleman stip forward an reckynised thim wid horrow—museer and Larry Mulvaney.

The latter seen us at the same time, and he cum smiling frum eer to eer up to Mr. Dudley, while the yung cupple stud still wid hands in aich uthers, looking wid smiling faces at their fathers, joost as if indade they were arfter ixpicting us.

"Mr. Dudley" ses Larry, "ye'll not be haulding it aginst me for me thrick. I boasted" ses he, "that I cud beet the Frinchman, and I did" ses he, "me frate being lite. It was no brake down ye were arfter being in on the road" ses he "I simply doomped ye there" ses he "to guv the yung fokes time. Besides" ses he "Delia there made a hyer bid for me sarvisses. All the welth in the warld" ses he, "cuddent bye me frum me pinnyliss darlint."

Mr. Dudley's silint, but he kipt his eyes stiddily on the yung fokes, then suddintly he hild out his hand to Mr. Wolley.

"I'm afrade sir" ses he, "that *love* has won the race."

Mr. James was acting strayngely. He wint down the isle in harf a dussen strydes. He brort his hand down wid a thoomp on Mr. Harry's back; then he toorned on his sister and guv her a smacking kiss.

"Claire!" ses he "ye've made me insanely happy."

She smiled, and Mr. Harry guv a larf.

"I oonderstand auld chap" ses he, "and heres a bit of prudint advice. Do as I did, tak the first steemer which will carry you her-wurds."

"By jove I will!" ses Mr. James, "I'll accipt the London corryspondint job to-morrow."

By this time the hole family is crowding about the yung fokes, and Mr. Dudley is after kissing the bride and bridegroom too, and both he and Mr. Wolley look as ef they'd blow there noses hard, but seeing there in choorch it might not be perlite.

The teers run down me nose, and wan of thim sploshed on Larry's hand, for I seen him look at it a moment. Then he wispered in me eer.

"Come, auld girl" ses he, "hop into the little masheen, which is joost around the corner. Maybe" ses he, "we can injuice sum sinsible praste to do us a like favour to-nite."

And so we wint sneeking out thegither, wid only the Frinchman to observe us, and he wid his mouth gaping open and smiling a bit beside, for Mr. Harry do be arfter giving him the hole of me forchune to act as witniss.

"But don't you be arfter wurrying swatehart" ses Larry Mulvaney, "for tho ye're puir yersilf now darlint, its a ritch man I'll be air long, wid the grand promisses of Mr. Harry."

"Ah, go wan Larry Moolvaney," ses I, giving him a squaze of his arm, "it's oanly a bit of a trick I've been playing you, me wanting to tist yere love fur me, or me wilth—Shure it was oanly a loan I'm arfter making Mr. Harry, and it's hivvy intrust the lad will be arfter paying on me savings," ses I.

A Note About the Author

Winnifred Eaton, (1875–1954) better known by her penname, Onoto Watanna was a Canadian author and screenwriter of Chinese-British ancestry. First published at the age of fourteen, Watanna worked a variety of jobs, each utilizing her talent for writing. She worked for newspapers while she wrote her novels, becoming known for her romantic fiction and short stories. Later, Watanna became involved in the world of theater and film. She wrote screenplays in New York, and founded the Little Theatre Movement, which aimed to produced artistic content independent of commercial standards. After her death in 1954, the Reeve Theater in Alberta, Canada was built in her honor.

A Note from the Publisher

Spanning many genres, from non-fiction essays to literature classics to children's books and lyric poetry, Mint Edition books showcase the master works of our time in a modern new package. The text is freshly typeset, is clean and easy to read, and features a new note about the author in each volume. Many books also include exclusive new introductory material. Every book boasts a striking new cover, which makes it as appropriate for collecting as it is for gift giving. Mint Edition books are only printed when a reader orders them, so natural resources are not wasted. We're proud that our books are never manufactured in excess and exist only in the exact quantity they need to be read and enjoyed.

bookfinity™

Discover more of your favorite classics with Bookfinity™.

- Track your reading with custom book lists.
- Get great book recommendations for your personalized Reader Type.
- Add reviews for your favorite books.
- AND MUCH MORE!

Visit **bookfinity.com** and take the fun Reader Type quiz to get started.

Enjoy our classic and modern companion pairings!